Rali

one of
the window
books

Translated by Margaret Roberts
Illustrated by Liljana Dicheva

Harrisburg, Pennsylvania

Rali

Stefan Dichev

STACKPOLE BOOKS

English language rights by
STACKPOLE BOOKS
Cameron and Kelker Streets
Harrisburg, Pa. 17105

First published in English in 1968
© 1961 Stefan Dichev
Copyright Protection Agency
11, Slaveikov Square, Sofia

Arrangements for English language rights
from the Bulgarian made by
Jerome Leavitt Publishing and Educational Services

Library of Congress Catalog Card Number 68-15493
Printed in U.S.A.

TO MY SON

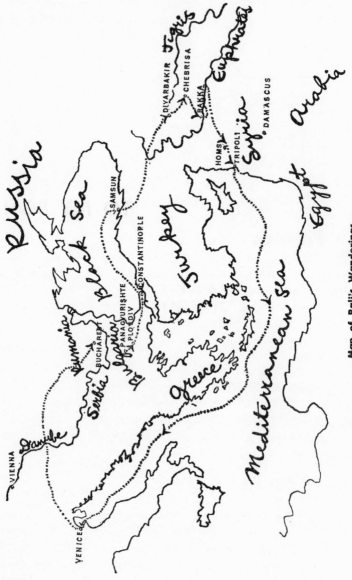

Map of Rali's Wanderings

Preface

RALI, WHO TELLS OF HIS WANDERINGS IN AN EFFORT to free his brother from a Turkish prison, was a Bulgar. The Bulgars were among the many different peoples—Greeks, Armenians, Gypsies, Arabs, Tatars or Tartars, Circassians, and others—who made up the great part of the Ottoman Empire of the Turks.

It was an empire that sprawled over eastern Europe, extending from the Black Sea to the Albanian Mountains and from the Danube River to the Aegean Sea, and reached into Asia and North Africa. It was the greatest of the empires of Islam, the religion founded by the Prophet Mohammed, whose followers were called Moslems or, more properly, Muslims.

The Ottoman Turks, descendants of the Turkish clan of Osman, were Moslems, as were a majority of the peoples in their empire. Although Islam was the state religion, the many Christians, such as the Bulgars, the Druses, and other groups, were allowed to practice their own religions. To the Moslems, those of other faiths were simply "infidels."

Not one language, but many different languages were spoken. The Bulgars spoke Bulgarian, a southern Slavic tongue. Most of the Gypsies, who were to be found everywhere in the realm, spoke their ancient Indian language. The Turks themselves spoke various Turkish languages, and there was no end to the number of dialects used by peoples speaking the same basic language, for instance, Arabic, Persian, or Turkish.

These peoples of different languages and different faiths, living in their various territories, were under the rule of the Turkish sultan at Constantinople, today's Istanbul. The Bulgars frequently referred to it as Tsarigrad, that is, the city (grad) of the emperor (tsar, tzar, czar—one has a choice of spelling). The sultan's power was wholly dependent upon military force and, during the hundreds of years that the Ottoman Turks held sway over a vast domain, no sultan was ever able to form a union of all the separate and hostile peoples whom the Turks had conquered.

Bulgaria had been an important nation before its conquest by the Ottomans towards the end of the fourteenth century. Under Turkish domination the spirit of its people had been crushed, and only once at the end of the sixteenth century had the Bulgars made a concerted endeavor to revolt, although the *haiduti* or outlaws in the mountains carried on for five centuries a kind of continual guerrilla warfare against their conquerors.

When Rali was a boy, the unwieldy empire was decaying. As its power declined, Turkish rule became more cruel and oppressive. In 1875, organized and resolute uprisings began in territories around Bulgaria. These were put down with extreme severity and at such great cost to an already heavily in debt government that the empire was almost bankrupt, its resources almost exhausted. The next year, outbreaks against the Turkish authorities spread to Bulgaria.

Fourteen-year-old Rali begins the story of his adventures one day early in 1876 at the time his father, older brother Lukan, and other rebels of the town of Panagyurishte, which was in the heart of the mountain country where Bulgarian nationalist feeling was strong, were helping to organize a general revolt.

Contents

The Sad Circumstances in Which I Introduce Myself

MY NAME IS RALI, AND AT THE TIME WHEN THIS STORY begins I had just turned fourteen. I was very tall and thin for my age, with a heavily freckled face, tousled hair and restless eyes—in short, a boy who could not yet be called a man but was no longer a child. I attended the local secondary school where my brother Lukan was a teacher, and I may as well admit from the start that I was not a keen student. I was always wanting to be out of doors, playing in the street with my friends or in the fields with the horse and my dog Balyu.

Actually the games we played at that time were no different from the main occupation of the adults. It was the beginning of 1876—an unforgettable year for those of us who survived. In my home town of Panagyurishte—and in the neighboring towns and villages I happened to visit with my father (as a wool buyer he often traveled over the Sredna Gora mountains and the lower Balkan plains)—in fact, everywhere—one could sense the same tension among the Bulgarians, the same ferment of secret preparations for the day we were all waiting for. Everyone was whispering about and planning for the uprising that was to rid our long-suffering nation once and for all of the cruel tyranny of the Ottomans.

We boys were not to be outdone by our fathers and older brothers. Besides, who had time for school any more?

Our games had turned into genuine battles. We had made ourselves wooden guns, used old sickles as yataghans,* and felt rich in the possession of a few rusty, dilapidated pistols. We would drive out the Turk at last! We would restore the long-lost Bulgarian State! That was all we could talk or think about. The rebel songs that were sung at home behind bolted doors came out into the open with us, and it was strange that there was no policeman to hear us and guess what was brewing in Panagyurishte. Perhaps the passing Turks saw everything but their proverbial laziness prevented them from sending for the Mutesarrif* in Plovdiv. But, looking back on it, I now suspect that they simply did not grasp what was going on. For them the slave was a slave—obtuse, uncomplaining, timid, and infinitely patient. True, from time to time rebel bands had been seen in the Balkan mountains, but what were a few haidouks* compared to the millions of soldiers at the Padishah's* command! Let the infidels parade about; let their children shout . . . If they really planned to revolt, that would be a different matter!

Yet that "different matter" actually came about. It came like a thunderbolt, like a tornado sweeping all before it and leaving only ashes and ruins in its wake.

After the first few days of the uprising, when people hugged one another and wept for joy, came the sober reckoning. What! Are these all the weapons we have? was the stunned question. And is it true that no one is stirring in the Sofia region, that no rebel flag is flying north of the Balkan Range and that the long-awaited reinforcements from Wallachia are not coming? Instead of news of relief, very different reports

---

*When an unfamiliar foreign word occurs for the first time in the story, it is followed by an asterisk (*) which indicates that its meaning is given in the Dictionary of Turkish, Bulgarian, Arabian, and Other Foreign Words at the back of the book.

reached us—the Sultan's troops were approaching on all sides, with the bashi-bazouks* close behind them. Then even we young ones understood that our rejoicing had been in vain and that now not freedom but annihilation and death awaited us.

To tell the truth, I cannot remember exactly what I felt during those days and hours. I only have a dreamlike recollection of the Turkish battalions advancing wave upon wave, and of our men crying, "We're out of gunpowder!" "We're surrounded!" "Don't give up, fellows!" "Freedom or death!"

Then the cannons started firing, bullets whistled through the air, houses caught fire (I kept looking to see if ours was burning too), then shouts and carnage . . . Suddenly, as if the floodgates had been opened, the Turkish soldiers swarmed into the town, and with them the bashi-bazouks. Then the horrors really began.

No! I can't remember. I don't want to remember! I learnt that my father, God rest his soul, had been one of the first to fall. They hacked him to pieces and I could not identify him afterwards among the hundreds of bodies. And my mother, I was told later, had barricaded herself in with my sister Petra in my grandmother's living room and they had all been burnt alive when the savage bashi-bazouks had set fire to the house.

By that time I had armed myself with our axe and was running from one position to the next in search of my brother's unit. Lukan was in command of a hundred men and carried a revolver and a sword. I felt that it would be safer where he was and that I should be with him at this critical moment when everyone around me was fleeing in panic and the whole world was falling apart. I finally found him—or, to be precise, not I but my dog Balyu scented him out and started bounding towards him. Just at that moment a band of bashi-bazouks came charging between us and my brother's decimated unit. There was a thunderous roar of gunfire, which scattered us in all directions, and when the smoke cleared away I found myself all alone. Ahead there was shooting, and behind me lay the town in flames. Dear God, what would happen now? What

➤ 13

would become of me? And what of my mother and Petra?—I suddenly thought, not yet knowing their fate. Which way should I go, where should I look for them? I could only cry and wander about like a lost, frightened animal. If only mother and Petra had escaped—if only they were in hiding! And if only Lukan was safe too!

I found myself back in the town among the burning houses. Could *that* be our house, with the black flames beating about in the wind, the smoldering piles of rubble? And my mother and little sister—where were they?

Just then I heard a call in Turkish behind me. I understood the language very well, having travelled so much with my father around the Turkish villages, but I was too frightened to make out a word. I started in terror as another voice thundered at me and, without looking round to see who it was, ran off as fast as my legs could carry me. Shots rang out. Then came another shot—the last one—and, just as I was turning off into the first side street, something hit me, and I felt a searing pain in my left arm above the elbow. I began to run even harder, and could think of nothing except that I must run faster and faster. After that I remember nothing.

When I came to, it was night. I opened my eyes and gazed at the stars above me and, as I did so, I had a sudden feeling that I was not alone. Someone was prowling about. I could hear his soft footfall and breathing, but I was so weak from loss of blood that I could not even register fear. Suddenly something wet and warm licked my face. Something shaggy—a wolf? I started up in alarm but was greeted with a joyful whimper. Two paws were planted on my chest and from that unexpected display of affection I recognized my dear faithful friend, Balyu.

I shall not describe my subsequent experiences—how I was found by a kindly couple who treated me with herbs and how I nearly died of grief soon after, on learning that I had lost my entire family. For days on end I was unable to believe the news. I hung about the lifeless town, which the Turks had abandoned after carrying away everything that could be removed. Here and there I came across homeless waifs like myself. We asked each other for news of our relatives, and of what was happening in the nearby villages and more distant towns. None of us was in a position to know anything at that time. We exchanged sympathetic glances and then wandered off, driven by our sorrows, until each of us returned to his own deserted courtyard and the ruins of his home. On reaching mine, I raked the ashes where our house had once stood, and wept. I was beyond consolation.

In the meantime more and more people were quietly reappearing in town. Where had they been hiding until now? In the mountains, perhaps. They came back frightened, searching for their relatives and their homes. What scenes I saw! A mother who had lost her children, a father who had lost his wife, a man without any arms, and others with burns from the smoking ruins. And who was responsible for all this? The Turk! That age-old villain of villains! Oh, how I hated them one and all—from the beggar-fanatic to the Sultan!

At that time I still had hopes that my brother Lukan might also reappear. I heard that his company had been tracked down and defeated. Nevertheless I kept telling myself that surely at least my brother was left alive. And this expectation helped me to forget my sufferings and woes.

Although it was the end of May, the weather had turned cold and to make matters worse I hadn't even a crust of bread (indeed, who had?). If it had not been for the small gardens on the outskirts of the town, and for the sloes, the sorrel, and the goosefoot, I would have starved to death. And I should not have been the only one!

Three weeks later my aunt Tanasa suddenly appeared with my cousins Rainichka and Hinko. They had been taking shelter with the villagers up in the mountains, and once again it took Balyu to recognize them, so emaciated and changed had they become in that short space of time. But it was not I who was taken aback at the sight of them.

"Rali, my poor boy!" my aunt cried and clapped her hands in dismay. "Look at you! Where is your father? And your mother?"

Where indeed? I choked back my tears. They were deep in the ground, and Petra with them, and perhaps even my brother. And I would never, never see them again.

I went to live with Aunt Tanasa. Their house had only been half destroyed and they also had a hidden supply of flour (they are the sort that hides everything). And the four of us somehow managed to organize ourselves and survive. Aunt Tanasa was one of the few townspeople who had not lost a single relative in the massacres. Her husband, like my father, was a cloth dealer, but he had a store both here and in Tsarigrad.[1] It so happened that two or three months before the uprising he had left for his other store and my aunt need have no fear on his account. Nevertheless she continually moaned, "What a state the Hadji* must be in (Uncle Doino had been on a pilgrimage to Mecca some years earlier), hearing of these horrors which are enough to make even God quail!"

She wept so noisily that passers-by shook their heads pityingly on hearing her wails. They must have thought that, like the other people in Panagyurishte, my aunt was mourning some irretrievable loss.

But, in spite of everything, by the end of the month most people had become inured and resigned. I noticed this in myself.

My family became a memory and I gave up hope of my brother's return, for I was so absorbed in my everyday needs that I thought only of where the next meal would come from. From early morning I was out in the gardens, digging and watering. Or Hinko and I would do repairs on the house. In the evening I would meet some of my school friends who had survived. But we no longer thought about our old games. We could only talk about what had happened, how it had happened, and how different things might have been if Russia— a name that was being whispered more and more often—had given us a helping hand.

"You know," said my friend Stanoi one evening, "my cousin Dobri has just come from Plovdiv and he told me . . ."

---

[1] Tsarigrad: Constantinople, today's Istanbul.

—here he lowered his voice—"that the Russian Tsar told the Sultan: 'Enough of this! If your zaptiehs* continue to hang Bulgarians it will be the worse for you, remember that!' "

We were all excited by this news. It was already being said that the Turks, not satisfied with having drowned the uprising

in blood, were going from village to village rounding up the rebels who had escaped them during the fighting. The prisons at Plovdiv were full to overflowing. Stanoi had even learnt from his cousin that some of the prisoners were men from Panagyurishte who had been caught by the search parties in the Sredna Gora mountains.

"From Panagyurishte?" I can still remember how my heart pounded at that moment. "Didn't he say anything about my brother? Didn't he hear if he was there or not?"

Stanoi looked away, and it may have been that involuntary movement that made me grab him with both hands.

"Stanoi! You know, but you won't tell me. Tell me, Stanoi, please! Don't torment me!"

"I don't know, Rali."

"Don't know! I understood you. You do know."

He turned his head, pondered for a while, and I noticed that his lips had gone dry. Then he said, "Dobri told me there was a teacher among them."

"It's my brother!"

"No, it's not. He doesn't know his name. Besides, Rali, don't raise your hopes. That's why I didn't want to tell you. You remember what I said about the hangings and the Russian Tsar. The zaptiehs were still hanging people. The whole town was lined with gallows, from the bridge to the Djumaya Mosque."

I had visited Plovdiv with my father a year ago and, suddenly, I could clearly picture the bridge over the Maritsa River, with corpses dangling from every telegraph pole. As far as the mosque? Dear God, suppose my brother was still alive and they were now about to hang him!

"Where, what prison is he in?" I stammered. "Does he know which prison the teacher is in?"

Stanoi told me all he could, and that very same evening I went to see his cousin Dobri, but I learnt no more from him. He could not even remember the name of the prison. He only told me that you came to it just after crossing the bridge. That was enough for me. I would go there. I had to go! But how? I hadn't a penny and Plovdiv was a long way off.

Again Aunt Tanasa came to the rescue. In one of her innumerable hiding places she found two liras* for me, and after going the rounds of the neighbors and explaining why I needed to get to Plovdiv as quickly as possible, I even found someone to lend me a horse.

Sometimes in time of trouble, people really become people and do a good turn which you remember all your life.

Early in the morning I said goodbye to all the family that was left to me, mounted my horse and set out for Plovdiv. What would I do when I arrived there? What could I do to help? I didn't even know myself. At the bend in the road when I turned round to take a last look at my unhappy little home town, where my parents and sister slept never to awake again, I was surprised to see an old and trusty friend following me—my dog Balyu. When he saw me looking back, he gave a happy whine and bounded along the roadside to join me.

"Let's go!" I shouted, spurring on the horse, and off we sped towards Plovdiv.

Part I
On the Trail

Chapter 1

Inquiring and Searching

WHEN I REACHED PLOVDIV THE SUN WAS UP ABOVE the Sahat Hill and from the minarets the muezzins* were announcing the second prayer.

The town presented a truly terrible sight.

The line of gallows started right at the beginning of the bridge. Every twenty paces there was a gallows. The livid corpses swung leadenly to and fro and a sickening smell filled the air. The swollen river rumbled below.

I distinctly remember slowing down the horse and searching the faces of the victims. I trembled as I looked, fearing all the time that I would catch sight of my brother's pale face, blond forelock and sandy moustache. Throughout that dreadful experience I kept saying to myself, "Supposing it is the next one? Oh, if only it isn't!" The gallows stretched endlessly one after the other and I could not rest until finally, faint with fatigue and drenched in cold sweat, I had inspected them all.

On the other bank, behind the low-roofed taverns, there

was a large pink konak.* Armed policemen were tramping in and out of it.

Ranged about the square were stalls with various delicacies and there was a smell of roast mutton and sharlan.* But I merely tugged at the horse's bridle, looked round and tried to locate the prison that Stanoi's cousin Dobri had spoken of. It must be somewhere around here. But where? And I set off to explore the side streets again until it occurred to me that it would be better to ask someone.

To ask was easy in theory, but ask whom? I saw no Bulgarians, only Turks. It was true that I knew their language well. There was no Turkish quarter in Panagyurishte, but as I already mentioned at the beginning of my story, my father and I had travelled quite a bit around their villages. But could I bear to approach a Turk? I hated them. And that was not all. I had seen the unreasoning and savage venom with which passing Turks glared first at me, then looked at my horse.

Finally, I couldn't bear it. Whatever the consequences, I could wait no longer.

"Aga,"* I addressed a thick-set, sullen man, wearing a green turban, "excuse me, aga, I am a stranger here. Where is . . ."

But he would not let me finish my sentence. Cursing and swearing, he shook his fist at me and walked on. My heart sank but I did not give up. I stopped another—a stout man with a small pig's eyes, gleaming with mockery and darting in all directions.

"Get off your horse before you speak to an Ottoman!" he reprimanded me, tugging at my leg.

I must confess that I was afraid as I got down, not for myself but for the horse. It was someone else's, and I knew what could happen.

"Ha! That's better!" The fat man uttered an unpleasant laugh and, when I least expected it, turned his back on me and walked away.

Leading the horse by the bridle, I set off again at random. I asked yet another man and he listened quite kindly, but he turned out to be a stranger to the town, and merely shrugged his shoulders.

I passed the pink building again. From the high-walled courtyard came the wailing of a zourla.* Someone was shouting in Turkish, "Beat him! Beat him!" And the sound of thrashing could be heard. Could this be the prison, I wondered. No, with those wooden columns supporting the jutting upper story and the flag flying over the entrance, the house looked more like a mutesarrif's konak.

I wandered on. I met some Turkish women who looked me up and down, their eyes gleaming suspiciously through the slits in their yashmaks.* Turkish children put out their tongues at me. One of them—a barefoot, snotty-nosed urchin —hit me with a lump of dry mud. Seething with anger, I was about to go for him; then I thought of my brother and my anger passed.

But Balyu took a different view of the matter. He chased the little Turk, and for a long time the narrow alley with its overhanging houses echoed with his furious barking.

"Come here!" I called when the Turkish boy had run away and hidden behind the houses. "We're going to find Lukan. We've *got* to find him!"

I had barely gone twenty paces when I met two Bulgarians —an elderly, stooping couple. The old woman could scarcely hobble along, and I remember that tears were trickling down her face, which was as shrivelled as a withered apple. The old man looked morose and tapped the cobbles with his stick, pausing now and then for her to catch up, and mumbling indistinctly. I do not know why, but the moment I saw them I couldn't help thinking, "They are looking for somebody too." They did not look like local people, but I decided that they knew where the prison was. I took off my cap and, holding the reins with my other hand, stopped in front of them.

"Excuse me, good people," I said. "I am looking for the prison. I have a brother there. Can you tell me where it is?"

The old man's stubbly face quivered and puckered. A curious look came into his eyes as he sized me up from top to toe. He was about to reply, but just then the old woman began to weep and moan, curses mingling with her laments: "May God slay those heathens. May they have no peace in the next world," she wailed until her husband stopped her.

"Quiet, woman, that's enough! Have some shame in front of that child! Can't you see that we are not the only ones?"

He did not say whether they were grieving over a son or a grandchild, but merely told me which way to go in order to find the prison ("that's where we have come from"). There was so much suffering in his voice that, without knowing why or how, I kissed their hands and quickly went off in the direction they had indicated.

I walked along, leading the horse, and my heart grew heavy with foreboding. Would I find out anything? What would I find out? And would I be able to do anything once I knew? I quickened my pace, thinking all the time, "What can I do?" And I could not get the old man's words out of my mind: "Can't you see, we are not the only ones."

* * * *

When I first saw the prison in the distance, it seemed a tiny, broken-down building with its lopsided roof just showing above the sagging outer wall. The first impression gave me hope. I thought, "My brother can escape." But I must confess now, after all these years, that for a moment I was also a little disappointed. In my imagination the prison had assumed gigantic proportions. I had pictured it as some sort of fortress, enclosed by massive walls. I had expected to see an entire battalion of guards posted at the entrance. Instead, there was one zaptieh squatting outside. He was leaning on his rifle and, at first, I thought he was asleep.

And there was something else that surprised me.

The little square in front of the prison and the side streets leading off it were teeming with people, who had come with carts, horses, donkeys or on foot. They must have been there for a long time, because they were standing quietly and patiently outside the gates. Most of them were country people from the surrounding villages, no doubt, and mainly men. There were few women's kerchiefs to be seen, and those were the black kerchiefs of the older women, like the woman I had met. Indeed, how could a young woman venture out in times like these we were living through!

In front of the cafe, which was at the near end of the square, a group of turbaned Turks were sitting cross-legged, with knives and pistols protruding from their belts. They suddenly started up from their mat and began shouting abuse at the cowed Bulgarians around them.

"Hey there, old rake!" I heard one of the Turks shout. He must have been addressing the tall, bareheaded peasant who was harnessing his oxen, evidently getting ready to leave.

"Here, old scarecrow! Wait a while! Where are you off to in such a hurry? The others will be hanged tomorrow. Stay and see the fun. After that we may hang you too!"

The other Turks hooted with laughter. The hushed square rang with their voices.

"Take a look at him, effendiler.* That brat there with the horse!"

This was obviously a reference to me, and I hastily hid behind the nearest carts. But the Ottoman kept shouting, "What do you want here, fellow? See, he's even brought his dog along! Let's take his horse away. What next? Even their children have started prancing about on horseback!"

In spite of his terrible threat, I saw out of the corner of my eye that he was not getting up from the mat. Nor were the other Turks. Thank God for their indolence! It saved my horse and helped in all the things which happened later and changed the course of my whole life!

A minute later I was mingling with the crowd, making my way across the square. As I was still afraid that they might catch me, I made for the prison.

The guard was still squatting there, leaning on his gun, the bottom of his baggy trousers reaching to the ground. I now saw that he was not asleep. He was chewing pumpkin seeds, with a dull, obtuse expression on his face.

I plucked up courage and said, "Aga, I am told that my brother Lukan, the schoolteacher from Panagyurishte, is a prisoner here. Have you heard of him, aga? Is he here?"

He went on chewing his seeds and from the look on his pimply face I realized that he was not listening.

I felt tears come to my eyes. My voice faltered as I shouted, "I'm asking about the teacher from Panagyurishte! Do you hear me? Do you know him?"

He turned his head, spat the husks of the seeds in my face and thundered, "Be off!"

"Try to remember, aga. His name is Lukan. He's from Panagyurishte! About so tall . . . and blond. He looks like me. He's a teacher, aga, a learned man. You can tell from his appearance." I would not leave him in peace.

"What do you want from me? Eh? There are two hundred prisoners in there. You'll see him when they hang him. What's your hurry?" And he went back to his seeds and forgot about me.

When I heard him say this, I felt a strange constriction about my heart and a painful ringing in my head. I think that I would have suffered less if I had seen my brother shot that time in Panagyurishte when we were counting the living rather than the dead. At least there would not have been that terrible, hopeless dread which held me in an icy grip and made me forget where I was and that there were dozens of other people, standing silent as phantoms nearby. Only now do I understand why, when I first saw them, they had seemed strange, lifeless and remote. I had become like them too, obsessed with a single thought, with fear of what was about to happen before my very eyes.

I sat down at one end of the square, the end furthest from the cafe with the Turks. The horse was wheezing beside me and breathing down my neck, while Balyu had curled up in my lap and lay motionless. Dear dog—even now I am sure that he sensed what was going on inside me and suffered with me.

I do not know how long I sat there, sunk in reverie. Then suddenly I felt a tap on my shoulder.

I lifted my head with a start.

A young man in a faded fez and shabby civilian clothes, with a blue ribbon round his neck, was bending over me. I remember his appearance as clearly as I remember his face, which was animated and tense. It stayed in my mind because at first I almost exclaimed aloud—he reminded me so much of my brother, of whom I was thinking, although he bore no physical resemblance to him.

The stranger said, "I heard you asking about Lukan the schoolteacher from Panagyurishte."

I jumped up, full of hope.

"Sir, do you know something? Is he in the prison?"

He did not reply but gave me an even more searching look.

"What is your name?" he asked unexpectedly.

"Rali."

"Rali . . . Yes, I remember that was his young brother's name."

"I am his brother, sir. I . . . I am the only one left . . . I
. . . They killed my father, and my mother, and my little
sister."

I choked back a sob.

"My brother Lukan is all I have left in the world, the
only person," I repeated. "If they kill him too, what shall I
do all alone?"

He laid his hand on my head. "Don't cry, Rali. Your
brother will not be hanged."

"Then he's alive?"

He nodded, gave me an encouraging smile, then, after
looking to see if anyone was approaching, told me that Lukan
really was in the prison.

"There are at least two hundred of our fellow countrymen
in there. Don't be misled. It looks small, but its dungeons are
deep," he said.

He took another quick look around and whispered, "Listen
now, Rali. But keep quiet about it! I know from a reliable
source that orders came from Tsarigrad last night to stop the
hangings. Russia insists. Do you understand, boy, Russia!
She says, 'Stop, or we'll make you.' "

I was speechless with joy and could only nod my head.
That was just what Stanoi's cousin had said! But then I
thought it strange—and I wonder about it to this very day—
the order had not come through when Dobri left Plovdiv.
So how had he known that the Russian Tsar was threatening
the Sultan? Or had it been wishful thinking? He believed that
it would happen because for centuries our people had believed
that one day Grandfather Ivan would come and free us forever
from the Turkish yoke.

"When will they let him out, sir? Does anyone know?" I
asked, plucking at the stranger's hand.

"Shh! Not so loud. Let him out? Be thankful that he is
escaping with his life! Now, now, don't look so downcast.
They are sending him to Diyarbakir."

I did not immediately grasp what he was saying.

"They are banishing him, boy. Perpetual banishment to
Diyarbakir! Have you ever heard that name?"

28 ◄

His voice started to falter, but he quickly pulled himself together.

"Don't lose heart! You know the saying, 'There's hope for a slave, but none in the grave!' That's how it is, Rali. These are the trials our people have to face. Those who are inside will suffer. Those who had the luck to stay out, like myself," he added, "have a job to do."

I listened to him, but I was thinking mainly of my brother. "Perpetual banishment," I whispered to myself. "Diyarbakir, life-long exile."

"Yes, my dear boy! But do you think we will stand for that? Remember, we still have our big sister Russia to hope in."

He patted my cheek and was about to leave when he suddenly asked, "Do you want to see him?"

Did I want to see him!

"Sir," I cried, "I would give anything to catch a glimpse of him!"

He hushed me and whispered, "Then be here tomorrow at dawn."

"I'll be here."

"No, not at this gate. Round the corner, there's another. Hide there so that the zaptiehs don't see you. Lukan will definitely be with the first batch of exiles. But don't go near them, or you may get hurt."

"All right, sir."

"Good then. Goodbye, Rali! You know, I've known you since you were so high," and he held his hand about three feet above the ground. "And now you're a tall lad. How old are you?"

"Fourteen."

"Fourteen," he repeated, and I noticed him thoughtfully taking in my face and my build. "You look older, you look strong. Be tough, Rali. Be fearless and bold! Don't despair, my lad. Remember what your parents died for. And don't forget whose brother you are! Goodbye again. Have you any money? Have you a place to sleep?"

"I have, sir."

"Then good luck, Rali. Have courage!"

➤ 29

He left me and was soon lost in the crowd of dejected people. I stood motionless for a long time, gazing at the spot where he had vanished. Who was this unknown well-wisher who had appeared at the most difficult moment in my life to encourage me? A friend of Lukan's. That meant he was from the Committee. That was why he had been to our house. And I had forgotten to ask him his name. But would he have told me? Anyway, what difference would his name make? Even without it I would always remember him. He was a Bulgarian, and that was enough for me.

Chapter 2

The Journey Starts

I SHALL NOT DESCRIBE WHERE I SPENT THE NIGHT or how. These details were obscured and forgotten in the anxiety that gripped me. What if I overslept? Suppose they took my brother away in the middle of the night?

Finally, I could bear it no longer and got up. Before daybreak I had already taken up my stand by the prison walls. They did not look so small and fragile now as they had during the day. Besides, guards with rifles on their shoulders were pacing about, their hobnailed boots clattering over the damp cobblestones.

Not daring to approach, I went round to a little back door (I had made quite sure where it was the day before) and began my vigil. But soon doubts began to creep into my anxious mind. Would the Mutesarrif really heed the order from Tsarigrad? Suppose, in spite of it, he said, "I'll hang this lot anyway, and see what happens."

All cruel, stupid and senseless questions, and how unworthy of me to doubt the assurances of my unknown benefactor! I began to go over them in my mind, pondering, worrying, tortured by the uncertainty. Suddenly I thought of something else—suppose they bring the prisoners out through the main gate at the front, instead of this little back door? I would not see my brother! I would never see him again.

I told Balyu to watch the horse and raced headlong down the side street to the front gate of the prison.

There everything was just as before. The lantern was shining over the sentry's head, although day had already dawned; the surrounding wooden houses still slept and only the empty square looked even more deserted, if possible, in the morning light. Then fears began to assail me again.

What if the little back door is opening now, I suddenly thought, and I was about to start back when the sound of horses' hoofs rang out in the street leading to the upper part of the town. The sound grew so deafening that it seemed to jolt the wooden houses to life with its reverberations. A minute later the little square was swarming with mounted policemen. Five . . . ten—no, eleven! But they did not stop. Their leader shouted something at the sentry, some such phrase as, "Is everything ready?" or "Hurry up there!" Then they turned their horses and rode off in pairs along the prison wall. They are making for the back door, I thought, and dashed off down the side streets by a roundabout route, hoping to arrive before them. I ran, slipped, fell, got up and started running again. My route was three times as long as theirs, and they were on horseback!

When I panted up to the spot where I had left Balyu and the horse, I found a dense ring of zaptiehs around the little back door. The street echoed with shouts, commands and oaths. But in the background there was another sound—the steady grating of iron on stone. It was the sound heard when the chain we used on our cart to secure the firewood came loose and dragged along the road. The same sound! But why is it the same, I wondered. Precisely because a chain was scraping against the wall, a chain was bouncing and rattling over the sharp cobblestones. And what a chain! Thick as a man's arm and sinuous as a snake! I saw it even before I

saw the wretched prisoners. There they came, chained together in single file. But where was my brother? I searched
the faces of the tattered, unshaven men as they filed out of
the little door. They were barefoot, unjacketed, with sunken
cheeks and feverish eyes. And the zaptiehs were lashing out
with their whips, striking anyone within reach. I saw an old,
bald-headed man stumble and fall, so that he was dragged
along by the chain. His companions tried to lift him up but
he only slumped more helplessly. "Get up, you dog!" bellowed
the nearest zaptieh, hitting him with the butt of his rifle.

I could not look at the scene any longer. I did not want to
see it. But where was Lukan? Just then Balyu shot past me
and darted between the legs of the policemen's horses.

"Here! Here!" I tried to stop him, but he disappeared into
the crowd. I heard his bark, joyful this time. Joyful? I ventured out of the sidestreet into the open. I looked all around.
There he was. There was Lukan! Unshaven, ragged, with
bruises on his face and blood on his shirt.

"Bate!"* I cried. "Bate Lukan!" And, faster even than
Balyu, I rushed between the zaptiehs towards him. Startled
by the sound of my voice, he turned round, looking everywhere for me. The chain hung from one of his hands.

"Rali!"

"Bate!"

He hugged me so tight that I could feel his heart beating,
boom! boom! boom! as if it were saying, "Rali! Rali!
Rali!" over and over again. The next minute the zaptiehs
were upon us. Something struck me in the face, and I felt
myself being flung aside.

"Bate!"

"Rali!"

From the ground where I lay, I saw them beating and goad-
ing him, saw him wave goodbye with his unfettered hand.
Then the houses swayed, spun round and toppled over, the
world came crashing down upon me and I lost consciousness.

When I came to, some men were bending over me. Their
voices, which at first sounded far away, gradually came nearer,
and finally dinned so loudly in my ears that I took them for

zaptiehs. I instinctively shrank back from them, expecting more blows. This reminded me of my brother.

Where was he? I lifted my head and feverishly scanned the street, peering between their legs. It was empty! These people were not zaptiehs.

"They've taken them away!" I groaned, and leapt to my feet.

The men looked at me. There were three of them and I now realized that they were speaking Greek.

"Wait, young man, you have blood on you," said one of them, trying to stop me. But I was already running towards the horse, springing into the saddle, digging my heels into its flanks.

"Where have they taken them?" I called, clutching the reins.

The one who spoke Bulgarian understood and pointed to the north end of the street. I spurred the horse and, quite forgetting to thank the Greek, galloped away.

Balyu was already well ahead of me.

* * * *

I saw the prisoners when I reached the Maritsa River. They had taken the Tsarigrad road going south from the bridge, along the riverbank, and it struck me somehow as eerie and horrifying that they should be filing, one by one, past the gallows with their dangling corpses. I reined in the horse. At this point the street led into an open square, and from there I kept my eyes riveted on the prisoners. I looked for my brother, trying to pick out his tall, slender form from among the others. But I couldn't find him.

I slowly started after them, not daring to go too close, and not lagging too far behind. I stopped whenever they halted for a rest, and moved on when they did. And so we left the town. By this time there were no more gallows—only a long, endless road disappearing into the distance.

To this day it is a mystery to me how, instead of taking the road back over the bridge to my home town, I came to be setting out after the train of prisoners. And they were going to far-off Diyarbakir! Supposing the zaptiehs had seen me. Would it have cost me my life? I don't know. I certainly never thought about it at the time. And I certainly could not have acted any differently. Apart from my brother I had nobody left and, if he, too, vanished from sight, I would be entirely alone in the world.

I cannot remember what villages we passed through that day. Our route was monotonous. Green plains ahead, the muddy waters of the Maritsa to our left, the undulating chain of mountains on the right. The sun was scorching; I had left my cap behind and the sweat was streaming down my forehead and neck. I had been too nervous in the morning to take a bite of food and by midday I was so hungry that, if I hadn't checked myself in time, I would have left practically nothing of the loaf of bread my aunt had given me when I set out. There was no need to worry about Balyu. He roamed the fields, hunting for hamsters and field mice, and digging up mole-hills. His belly was swollen with food. Twice he ran up to where the prisoners were sitting under the willows. At the last village the poor fellows had each been given a crust of bread, which they were chewing now, moistening it in water from the river flowing at their feet.

So much for my lunch and theirs. Then we set out again.

From the distance I had already taken stock of the entire party. There were fifty prisoners and eleven guards. Oh, if only a rebel band would spring out, right now, from the vineyards, I thought, picturing the shooting, the zaptiehs put to flight, the prisoners rending their chains and myself rushing to help my brother.

Alas! We left the vineyards behind. Again the bare green countryside stretched out on both sides—not a sign of life apart from an occasional peasant on a donkey or on foot, or a cart rattling along the road. I began to count again. There were fifty prisoners and only eleven zaptiehs. But where were the rebels? Where were our brave heroes? Who dared to raise his head after all the horrors and destruction?

It grew dark. Evening came. The zaptiehs unsaddled their horses and let them loose to graze in the fields. The prisoners lit fires and stretched out beside them.

I lay down between two bushes and, while my horse quietly champed the grass which was thick and luxuriant after the recent rains, I impatiently watched the fires gradually growing smaller and smaller. I could barely distinguish the forms of the prisoners, but the zaptiehs stood out clearly against the bright background of the flames. Occasionally there would be a glint from their guns, and voices could be heard shouting threats.

I planned to steal up to my brother when they were all asleep, so I lay there waiting, without knowing exactly what I would do, or how I would do it.

I do not know how many hours passed in this way, because there was no moon and only the stars glimmered overhead, before I finally decided that the time had come. I tied a length of twine round my dog's neck so that we would not lose each other in the dark, and we set off. To begin with I walked doubled over, but as we drew near I got down on my hands and knees and crawled. Thus, without making a sound, we skirted the nearest of the three sentries. Just then he gave a loud yawn. I saw that Balyu was about to bark and held his muzzle. Like the good, sensible dog he was, he just looked at me reproachfully and kept quiet.

"Find him!" I whispered in his ear. "Take me to Lukan!"

I do not know what other people think, but I am absolutely convinced that my dog understood everything I said to him. Before the uprising, when playing with my friends or at home, I had paid no attention to this, but now he and I were alone, and were suffering together for my brother's sake. For me Balyu was no longer just a sandy-haired, high-spirited dog with a pointed white nose, whom I sometimes scolded and even beat without just cause. He was now my only friend and helpmate in time of trouble.

We crawled past the nearest sentry, and threaded our way between the prostrate forms of the zaptiehs (for a moment I was tempted, and picked up a rifle, but my better judgement prevailed and I put it down again). Then, careful to keep away from the fire, we approached the prisoners. Poor things, they were sleeping on the bare ground, clad as they were in

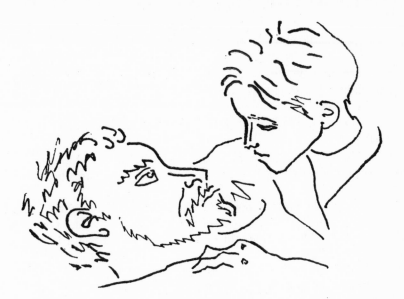

their shirts, one hand under their head, the other locked in the chain. In the darkness there seemed to be so many of them, all looking so alike, that if Balyu had not led the way I would never have been able to find my brother. When I finally discovered him among all those snoring, bearded men, I hesitated a moment. He had his face to the grass and was in the shadow. Moreover he was muttering in his sleep and his voice sounded unfamiliar. What if I woke the wrong one? What if he cried out?

I glanced at Balyu. He had stopped sniffing and seemed to be trying to say, "Look, I've found him. What are you waiting for?" I gently touched the sleeping man. He stopped muttering but did not awaken.

"Bate!" I whispered, tapping him again.

Before he turned his head, I saw him opening his eyes.

"What is it?"

He must have thought that one of his companions was waking him. Then he recognized me.

"Rali!" His first reaction was to look around for the guard.

"They didn't see me," I reassured him.

He hugged me and drew me down into the shadow. "What are you doing here? Why did you follow us?"

"I couldn't leave you, Bate, I'll never leave you!"

"Do you know where they are taking us? Have you thought what might happen to you?"

"I know."

"Go back, Rali! Who will look after mother if she falls sick?"

"She won't fall sick, Bate, nor will Petra. They were burnt to death. Everything is gone. Just you and I—we are the only ones left."

His whole body shook and he groaned aloud, unable to utter a word. Perhaps I should not have told him. Or, at least, I should not have told him just then. What could I do to comfort him?

"Don't worry," I said. "I'll help you escape."

"No, no. Stay out of it. It's certain death, little brother. Get away while you can. Go back to Panagyurishte, Rali!"

"No!" I insisted with a stubbornness I never knew I had in me. "I've made up my mind. I am going to rescue you from these brutes."

Then I thought of the piece of iron I had found in one of the villages we had passed through.

"Take this," I said, feeling for his hand in the dark.

"What is it?"

"An iron bar. Can't you use it to break the chain? I have a horse. By the time they notice you're missing, we'll be well away."

I saw that he was hesitating. But suddenly hope triumphed and he turned over, pulled the massive chain towards him with his fettered arm and poked the iron bar into a link. He pressed hard. The elbow of his free arm hit the ground.

"It's no good," he said dully. "The chain twists round."

"Wait, I'll help you."

"Be careful, you'll wake the others."

The others! I had not thought about them. Lukan was afraid that they might give us away. But was he right? I now think that he was wrong. If all the prisoners had banded to-gether, formed a bold, united front and attacked the sleeping guards with my help, their lives might have taken a different course. But by now they were frightened and broken men. Also, not many of them had known each other before.

I held the thick chain against the ground with both hands, putting my whole weight on it, while Lukan pushed the iron bar into the link.

"Are you holding it?"

"I'm holding it, push hard." As I spoke the chain, as a result of the pressure, shot out of my hands and turned over with a loud clank, jerking at the wrists of the two nearest prisoners. They sat up, muttering, but I did not hear what they said because just then the sound of the guard's voice froze me to the spot.

"Why aren't you sleeping, you scoundrels? What are you up to? Breaking the chain, eh?"

I heard footsteps. He was coming towards us.

"Run for it," commanded my brother.

I realized that I ought to run; instead I clung to him despairingly and whispered, "I won't leave you, Bate. I'll help you escape . . . I . . ."

"Run! Get away, I tell you!" He pushed me roughly away from him. It was well that he did, for I had barely crawled a few yards when I saw the guard's lantern swing nearby and stop at the very spot where I had left my brother.

"Here, show me the chain! Bring it closer!" I heard the zaptieh's harsh voice behind me, then the jangling of iron. Someone said something—it must have been my brother—but by then I was too far away to catch the words.

I covered another fifty paces in the dark and whistled for Balyu. But as usual he was at my heels. And he led me to the horse. I lay down again between two bushes, wrapped myself in my coat and gazed at the prisoners' fires in the distance. The sentry must have stoked them up, because the flames were twice as high as before. "They are sleeping on the bare ground," I thought to myself. "They haven't even a coat to put over them as I have. If only I had taken mine to Lukan!

But what if the guards saw it in the morning? I should have taken him my bread. Out of my two liras, I could have bought some more tomorrow at the next village." I felt so guilty that I was about to creep back to the camp, in spite of the brightly blazing fires, and take my brother the rest of my bread. Suddenly I remembered the impulsive promise I had made him—that I would set him free! We would return together to our native town, to our home and the school. What a model pupil I would be from then on, how studious and hard-working! I would do it!

"Yes, I will! I won't give up. I won't rest until I have carried out my promise!" I told myself as I lay there alone in the dark. And the crickets chorused their approval of my decision, telling me that everything is possible when one wants something as badly as I did. Eventually I fell asleep to their chanting, for it had been a hard day for me; I was only a fourteen-year-old boy.

Chapter 3

A Fateful Decision

A PERSON WILL SAY, "I HAVE MADE MY DECISION," without even suspecting the dangers and difficulties that he is inviting from that moment on. And it is just as well that he does not suspect. Otherwise, think of the conflict and anguish he would suffer the next day, when he realizes that many such days lie ahead, all equally tense and equally fruitless!

Actually, even if I wanted to, I would find it hard now to recollect in detail each day that followed that first unforgettable day. I rode after the train of prisoners, stopping whenever they did. At night I would try to steal up to the camp to find my brother, give him some bread and make another attempt at breaking the chain. But I managed only one more visit because the sentries suddenly became suspicious and kept the fires blazing brighter every night. Had they noticed that someone was prowling about in the dark? Or had they seen me following them at a distance? I do not know, but from then on I had to be very alert. My brother even lost his temper with me and said, "Don't come up here any more! If I can get free somehow, I'll come and find you myself."

Then there were days, depending on the area, when I was left so far behind the group that I could barely distinguish those on horseback from those on foot. Jogging along on my horse, I let my mind wander, dreaming of Panagyurishte and my friends, or of our home and the happy times we had there. My father, stern but always with a twinkle in his eye. And my dear sweet mother, God rest her, always fussing over us. And my little sister, Petra—her face was freckled, like mine, but she had a little turned-up nose that made you laugh, just to look at it. I would begin smiling to myself at the memory, then the tears would start to my eyes as I realized that all that was gone, vanished from the face of the earth.

Sometimes I was struck by other thoughts, which sent shivers down my spine. Where are we really going, I wondered, because I could only vaguely remember, from my school days, the map of Turkey and the names of the places we had to pass through to reach Diyarbakir. And there was another thing that worried me even more than my uncertainty about the route —money! I saw it dwindling day by day, and on the twelfth day (I remember it because just then we were passing through Adrianople) I hadn't an asper* left. What was I to do? It must be another hundred kilometers* to Tsarigrad, where I hoped to find Uncle Doino, my aunt Tanasa's husband.

I could not go very far without bread, so I sold the horse. It belonged to someone else, and I had promised to return it safely to its owner. Now here I was selling it, and for a mere song. I received four liras for it, although it was worth at least ten. But, I thought, if I only come back with my brother one day, we'll repay our neighbor, both for his horse and for his great kindness.

Now I had money, but had no horse, and faced the prospect of having to walk. Would I be able to do it? Would I last the journey? But think of the prisoners—and they had to carry a chain!

I bought myself a fez, because we were going through more and more Turkish villages and it was becoming dangerous to go bareheaded. I bought some bread, and a file, for I had a plan forming in my mind: I'd give the file to my brother! Excited and encouraged by this thought, I set off cheerfully after the prisoners. But very soon the weather turned rainy. The convoy now avoided sleeping in the open, and took shelter under the awning of some high-walled courtyard in the villages we passed through. Only Balyu and I would be left outside in the dark alleys, and always haunted by the same fears and the same loneliness which, alas, I could never get used to. Moreover, I had caught a bad cold. I sometimes thought that I would die like this, on foreign soil, with no one to know who I was or where I came from. Then to calm my fears I would hug Balyu close to me, stroke his shaggy head, feel his warm breath, and talk to him for hours in the dark, sobbing out all my woes to my one and only friend.

In this way another ten days went by. Then, one morning, the horizon ahead of us assumed strange and unexpected contours. From end to end stretched high stone walls, with hundreds and hundreds of minarets, shining domes and white turrets towering beyond them. I realized that we had finally reached Tsarigrad.

On passing through one of the gates in the large city wall I felt a curiosity and excitement that were hardly in keeping with my bad luck, still less with my hatred of everything Turkish.

The capital of the empire! Tsarigrad! How often I had heard that name!

To avoid losing the prisoners I went nearer, and stayed close behind them, listening by force of habit for the clanking of the chain, but (I am ashamed to admit) letting my eyes wander over the scene with avid curiosity. Houses, houses, so many houses—all built of wood and huddled together. They were several stories high and had two or three projecting eaves, which cast blue shadows and provided shelter from the blazing sun.

Through a gap in the houses I glimpsed the other side of the town in the distance, perched on a hilltop and dazzling white. Below, at the foot of the hill, was something blue, flat and sparkling. I recognized it immediately—it was the sea! Of course, I had never seen the sea, even in pictures, but I recognized it at once. It was just like the descriptions in books, and just as Lukan (who had studied at Odessa) had described it to me many times.

That must be a bay over there, I decided, automatically recalling my geography lessons and, strange to say, memories of school came flooding back to me with astonishing clarity. I felt as if I was right there in the classroom. Lukan was examining Spindly Stoiko, who, as usual, was floundering hopelessly and I was doing my best to prompt him. Stoiko was too terrified to hear me, but my brother heard, and I was made to kneel on grains of corn with my face to the wall. What a humiliating experience! He was my brother, wasn't he? Then why did he have to punish me? But he punished me precisely because he was my brother. That's the way he was—strictest on himself and on his nearest and dearest.

Suddenly I realized that those far-off days were gone and that I was standing there gazing at the sea. Where were the prisoners? Which turning had they taken? Seized with panic, I rushed off to find them. There was no sign of them in the nearest street. The next? Not there either! Oh God, where had they disappeared to! All those days I had not let them out of my sight, and now here, where I could safely have followed at their heels . . .

I went back to the crossroads. My terror and despair grew

with each moment that passed. What if they have gone into some building? Suppose they have been put away, and I shall never see again! I wanted to cry aloud with grief and from anger at myself.

I set off, trusting to chance.

Even in my despair I never thought, even for an instant, "There's nothing more for me to do here. I'll go back to Panagyurishte." Diyarbakir! Were it at the end of the world, I would go there.

Actually all these thoughts occur to me only now. At the time, I did not stop to think and was not even conscious of my feelings. I simply ran madly this way and that way, looking here, there and everywhere. Suddenly the sound of distant voices made me turn and glance down a side street. I saw . . .

But one thing at a time!

After a couple of hundred feet, the alley broadened out into a wide marketplace with dozens of little shops, shaded by tall Italian pines, and with multi-colored stalls piled high with wares of various kinds. But it was not the shops or the goods that caught my eye, but the convoy. The prisoners were trying to push their way through the dense mob of excited and angry Turks clustering round them. The Turks were shouting, waving fists, brandishing sticks and spitting at the unfortunate Bulgarians, and savagely pelting them with rotten fruit and garbage.

"Death to the rebels!" screamed several voices, the loudest coming from the shrill kadinas.*

I somehow found myself caught up in the crowd.

"Grab that young infidel there," someone shouted behind me. Someone else struck me, and a third person tried to grab me, but I slipped out of his grasp and, although I dropped my bag, I pushed safely through the crowd and emerged at the front, right by the zaptiehs' horses.

Here menacing shouts mingled ominously with the sound of lashing whips and the clank of chain. Where is Lukan, I wondered, looking round anxiously for him. I could not see him anywhere, not a sign of him. In despair, I ran between the convoy and the crowd, and nearly fell under the horses' hoofs, when suddenly a familiar warning bark made me turn my head.

Balyu!

Why hadn't I thought of him when I was chasing to and fro at the crossroads, when I had lost not only the trail but all hope as well? But he hadn't been anywhere around then. I turned round sharply, looking for him. Balyu saw me looking, uttered a joyful bark and, just as he had done at Plovdiv, darted between the policemen's horses to show me the way. Then I saw Lukan. He was carrying the heavy chain over his shoulder but, oddly enough, his long thin face with its growth of reddish beard showed no trace of its earlier suffering and desperation. On the contrary, he held his head high and his eyes blazed defiance. He marched confidently, looking straight at the wrathful crowd, as if to say, "Shout away! If you had your way, you would have hanged us all by now. But you are afraid. You are scared of Russia! One day she will pay you back for all our sufferings."

Suddenly he saw me. A tender, anxious look, which I had never seen before, came into his eyes. "You can't help me. Go away!" he seemed to say. I shook my head in dumb misery. "No, I won't go away" was my silent retort. "I am going to save you, Bate. Nothing can make me turn back now!"

That was the last conversation we had. After crossing the marketplace, the convoy filed off down a number of very narrow streets and I had to fall behind.

I have no idea how much ground we covered or where our route took us. I did not see the prisoners assembled together again until they halted in front of a massive iron gate at the end of a round piazza with torn-up paving. The high stone walls on both sides of the gate, the pointed tower and the guards at the entrance gave me the idea that this was a prison (I realized later that it was the main prison of Tsarigrad, the Metarkhana). I made my way there quickly and unobtrusively, but, before I could reach the gate, a crowd of curious onlookers barred the way. They hid the Bulgarians from view and, although I tried standing on tiptoe and jumping up and down, all I could see was the iron gate as it creaked open and swallowed up the convoy in its greedy jaws.

I was dimly aware of a voice beside me saying, "Those are the ones they were waiting for. They will spend the night here and tomorrow at noon, God willing, they will leave for Samsun on the *Osmanieh.*"

Another voice asked, "Are they for Diyarbakir too?"

"What else are they fit for? It's banishment for life!"

"Banishment for life!" I repeated in a daze, as if I didn't know where they were taking my brother, as if I didn't know that he would molder there in chains till the end of his days!

The onlookers began to disperse. I had to move away from the gate too, or I would be in trouble.

And now what? I would go and look for Uncle Doino. But what if the prisoners were taken out in the interval? Then, suddenly, the words I had heard a little while ago came back to me and lifted me out of my despondency. They had said that tomorrow at midday the prisoners would be taken to Samsun on the *Osmanieh. Osmanieh*—what was that? It must be a ship, because to the best of my recollection Samsun was a town, an Anatolian port on the Black Sea.

I called Balyu after me and walked away from the prison, with the words Osmanieh and Samsun still ringing in my head. Samsun? I was not a prize pupil in geography and, besides, as I said at the beginning of my story, during the months just before the uprising no one had felt like studying. However, I had often gazed at the map hanging in Lukan's room at home. He had brought it back from Russia, and I had often looked at it to see where Bulgaria was, how large the old Bulgarian State had once been, and where our masters came from. Now the name Samsun suddenly emerged from some hidden recess in my mind. I saw the shape of that strip of coastline in Asia Minor, the dot marking the town, just inland, and the thin black wavy line leading away from it—that was the road—and I clearly remembered the names Samsun, Sivas, Malatia, Diyarbakir.

My doubts all vanished. The pieces all fitted together, the picture was complete. The *Osmanieh* was the ship on which the prisoners would sail tomorrow at noon. Samsun was the port where it would stop, and from there stretched the long, terrible road to Diyarbakir.

Chapter 4

My Uncle Hadji Doino

THERE IS NO NEED FOR ME TO DESCRIBE IN DETAIL my wanderings in Tsarigrad—how I went to the harbor and discovered that there really was a ship called *Osmanieh,* and how I then roamed from marketplace to marketplace until, after walking for miles, I found my uncle's store. There is a saying that, if you ask often enough, you will even find your way to Constantinople, that is, Tsarigrad. But I should like to add that it is easier to find the capital city among all a country's towns and villages than to find the shop of Hadji Doino from Panagyurishte in all the bustle of Constantinople!

Anyway it must have been four or five o'clock—I no longer remember exactly—when dropping with fatigue, distracted with anxiety and close to tears, I finally stood before Hadji Doino.

He gave me a suspicious look out of the corner of his eye and seemed not to recognize me. A lump came to my throat.

"Uncle!" I whispered hoarsely. "Uncle, don't you recognize me? I'm Rali!"

"Rali?"

"Rali from Panagyurishte!"

He gave a start. "So it's you, Rali?" I noticed that he turned pale. "Where have you sprung from? What a sight you look, all tattered and muddy." His face assumed a sad, sympathetic expression. "There, there, my boy, I know all about it. I heard the news from your Aunt Tanasa. You have suffered a terrible misfortune, Rali."

I gave a loud sob and, before I knew it, the tears were rolling down my cheeks.

"It can't be helped. It's God's will. Come on in here." He led me into the back of his shop, then went to bolt the outer door.

"Now tell me," he said when he came back. "Your aunt wrote and told me that our house, too, was damaged by fire. But she didn't tell me anything about the shop. Is it all right? A good thing that I brought the stock here."

I told him what he needed to know and saw that he was reassured, so much so that he even began to deliver a lecture.

"I told them so. Those plans of yours won't do us any good, I said. But they wouldn't listen. They had to have an uprising. Now look what's happened! Your father, God save his soul, even he was a wild one. And your brother Lukan was worse."

"Lukan is here, Uncle!" I cried.

He stopped open-mouthed. His little squinting eyes gleamed with suspicion; there was a hint of fear in them too.

"Lukan?" he repeated slowly, as if trying to decide whether I was joking or not. "Here, you say. Is he with you?"

And I saw him glance quickly towards the door.

"No, no, he's in the prison. Tomorrow the prisoners are being taken to Diyarbakir, banished for life, Uncle."

I told him about the uprising, then about Plovdiv and how I had made my way here. While I was talking I could not help staring at my uncle's broad mustachioed face, at his paunchy figure, at his little fat hands, nervously tapping the beads of his rosary. I had heard my father say that Hadji Doino was a cowardly, unfriendly person, who was only out for his own interests. I could see this for myself now and was ashamed of him. I was also afraid that he would not help me.

"You are out of your mind!" he exclaimed. "Diyarbakir! Have you any idea what kind of a place it is?"

"I promised my brother. I am going to help him."

"Stop this childish nonsense! Look at you! How old are you? Fourteen?"

"I'm in my fifteenth year."

"Even if you were in your twentieth, there's nothing you can do. You are up against a powerful state, don't you realize that? Do you want to end up like Lukan now that he's got his deserts?"

"Uncle!" I jumped to my feet, my heart pounding furiously. How dare he speak like that about my brother, who had shed his blood for people like him and now had to face banishment for life? And he called himself a Bulgarian!

I remember—and the thought still fills me with shame— that even though at that moment I hated Hadji Doino, even though I loathed and despised him, a voice somewhere inside me warned me against an angry outburst. I bowed my head and sat down again on the sofa. No, it was not meekness, for I am not submissive by nature, and was much less so in those days. But the next day they were going to take the prisoners away on the *Osmanieh* and I needed money for a ticket to Diyarbakir, and for whatever was required once I got there. Who could give me the money but Hadji Doino?

"Uncle," I began and, from the humiliation and excite- ment, I wrung my hands so hard that my fingers went quite numb. "Uncle, you know, we have seven and a half acres of land in Panagyurishte."

He looked at me in surprise. "Well, what of it?"

"I want to sell them."

Hadji Doino raised his bushy eyebrows and scowled. He was thinking it over, calculating. I knew that buying and selling were his passion.

"So," he said, letting go of his beads and fingering his left mustache. "That's right, the property is yours now, and Lukan's. But he doesn't count. Listen, my boy, you are a child, you have no right to sell. Of course we might arrange some-

➤ 51

thing. But who is going to buy your land? How much do you want for it?"

"As much as you'll give."

He looked at me in alarm. I had guessed his thoughts.

"Who, me? Hm...I don't need any property, but...as you say...For your sake, since you're an orphan...."

Suddenly he stopped and looked at me, differently this time, suspiciously.

"What do you want the money for? To go after Lukan?"

"Yes, that's why," I answered firmly. "What good is the land to me, now that I have no one in the whole world except my brother? If I lose him, I've as good as lost everything."

Before I had finished speaking, Hadji Doino jumped up from his seat and started angrily pacing about the room. He was in a turmoil, torn between greed and fear. Obviously he was thinking: "I'll get his father's land dirt cheap—not a bad idea. But if the Turks catch him, and he lets out that I gave him the money, that I know . . ."

Finally he stopped in front of me. Before he started speaking, I knew that fear had gained the upper hand.

Emphasizing each word carefully, he said, "Listen to me, nephew. Tonight you can sleep here, but tomorrow you leave for Panagyurishte. And don't talk any more about that silly business, or I'll go straight to the police station," he threatened. "It's bad enough having to worry on account of one of you.

Be quite sure that I'll report you without a moment's hesitation! Don't imagine that I shall be an accomplice. Do you hear me? And don't move from my shop until tomorrow."

He went to unlock the door. While we had been talking, several customers had tried to enter.

I stayed on the sofa behind the partition, helpless with fury and disappointment. I could not find a single cheerful thought to comfort myself with.

Evening came, and I still had found no way out of my difficulty. We had dinner, and I must say, Hadji Doino regaled me handsomely. Then we lay down to sleep, he on the couch in the back room and I on top of the counter in the shop, between the shelves of woollen cloth. I was so worn out after the journey that I fell asleep immediately.

How long I slept, I do not know. Nor do I know what awakened me. Perhaps it was Balyu, who had curled up to sleep at my feet, as he had done all during the journey. Or I might have had a disturbing or frightening dream, because after that I could not get to sleep again.

It was a bright moonlit night. Through the wooden bars of the window looking onto the back garden peered the round face of the moon, as if carved into slices. I lay on the hard counter, tossing and turning and wondering what I ought to do. Go back to Panagyurishte without my brother? No, my heart counselled, not at any price. Then go on to Diyarbakir. But what about the ticket for the boat? I got up and took out the knotted handkerchief containing the money left over from the sale of the horse. I untied it and counted the coins—two liras and ten piasters.* Would that be enough for the ticket? Hardly. Besides, what would I eat, where would I stay when I reached Diyarbakir? And, most important of all, how would I help my brother to escape when I had nothing myself?

I put away the money, but my mind kept on turning over schemes. Wouldn't it be better after all to go back to Panagyurishte, sell my entire property and *then* go on to Diyarbakir? My brother would still be there. He'd been banished for life, hadn't he?

I lingered over this idea for a long time and, while I was considering it from all angles, I couldn't help hearing the snores that issued through the half-open door of the back room. Hadji Doino was no doubt dreaming of piasters and pieces of gold; yet he lived here like a hermit. What did he do with all his money? Where did he put it? Yes, where! He must hoard it in that cupboard over there. Yes, that was it! I had seen him the evening before when he hadn't known I was watching him. He had crouched down, looked over his shoulder, taken the leather purse out of his belt and put it in the cupboard. Then he had locked it up. The key of the padlock? Where was it? I tried hard to remember.

I got down from the counter and walked over to the cupboard in my bare feet. I could see it clearly in the moonlight, a heavy oaken cupboard, with a large padlock, impossible to open.

Actually, until that moment, it had not occurred to me that what I had in mind was theft. From my early childhood I had known that stealing was wrong. Turks stole and so did people like Hadji Doino, who bought cloth from the poor people of Panagyurishte for twenty piasters a bale and then sold it in Tsarigrad for a whole lira for one piece. What about me? Was the money for myself? No, it was for my brother, to free him from his chains. Besides, wouldn't we pay it back with interest to Hadji Doino one day?

We could pay it back in no time at all. Dare I . . . ?

I began to pace about the room. The floor creaked and I was afraid that my uncle might wake up, but he was snoring so loudly that the sound of my footsteps must have been completely drowned.

I opened the window and looked out onto the courtyard. It was not too far down. I could make out the shapes of some barrels, a boxwood hedge and, by the wall, a scattering of packing cases of the kind used for shipping fabrics. There was also a pile of refuse in which something glistened, probably glass.

It was a fine night, pleasant and warm.

I drew back, and was about to close the window when, just as I was taking hold of the two halves of the casement, I remembered exactly how Hadji Doino had closed the cupboard. He had snapped the padlock shut, half-turned his back to me, and fastened something to his watch chain. The key! In a flash I was at the door leading to the back room.

The door was ajar. I crept in on tiptoe. The floor creaked and my heart was pounding so hard that I seemed to hear it. In the half-dark I kept my eyes riveted on my uncle. Supposing he woke up? But he snored away, lying on his back on the low couch. Encouraged by this, I went over to the wall where his coat was hanging.

Its deep pockets contained a tobacco pouch, a flint, a bent nail and a piece of folded paper, but the chain with the watch and key was missing. I looked around. There was a shiny object on the little round copper pot. Where was the key? Under the pillow! Yes, I was certain it was under the pillow. That was just where Hadji Doino would put it, or keep it tied round his neck.

I slipped my hand under the hard pillow and slowly, very slowly, felt around. Any minute my uncle might open his eyes. Finally my fingers met something cold. The chain! I gave it a tug, then another little tug, and out it came with the flat Turkish watch and the key. An instant later I was at the cupboard. I put the key in the padlock and turned it. The padlock sprang open. I took it off and opened the doors of the cupboard with trembling hands.

What occurred after that seems like a strange dream. To this day I do not know and still cannot fathom how it happened that, the minute I opened the cupboard, a little bell started tinkling in the next room. Perhaps there was a hidden wire connecting it to the cupboard door. I heard a grunt, a shout and then a clatter. "He's waked. He'll catch me!" flashed into my numb brain. I snatched up the first little bag in sight, sprang for the window, squeezed head first through the wooden bars, stepped out and then . . . crash! I went hurtling into the boxwood hedge, by the pile of barrels. A good thing I didn't land on them, I thought, as I got up. Suddenly I felt a shove and fell over again, but my fright turned to joy when I saw that it was Balyu.

"Let's run for it," I whispered and ran towards the wall.

Hadji was already shouting from the window, "Stop! Drop the money or I'll shoot! Let go of the money!"

I leaped over the pile of boxes, with Balyu behind me. I snatched him up in my arms and threw him over the wall. I followed him over. A loud report rang out, awakening the sleeping neighbors. Was I hit? At first I did not know, because in my haste I had landed so awkwardly on the sharp cobblestones that I groaned with pain.

Hadji Doino's voice could still be heard shouting, "Stop thief! My money! Police, stop that ruffian, he's a rebel! Stop him!"

Windows began opening, and I could hear the rattle of firearms and the tramp of feet. Just as I had that time in Panagyurishte, when I was fleeing from the bashi-bazouks, I now sped down deserted side streets, forgetting both the pain and my fatigue. On I ran, dodging into doorways, cutting through overgrown ruins, constantly looking back and thinking that I was being followed.

In reality no one was following me except Balyu. I realized this only when I came to the sea and saw the large resplendent face of the newly risen sun smiling reassuringly at me from the opposite shore of Asia Minor.

Chapter 5

I Follow Levsky's Example

I MUST CONFESS THAT I FELT STRANGE AS I UNDID the bag of money. I was sitting by the seashore, safe from curious eyes, but still I didn't dare to look inside. Perhaps it had all been for nothing. The bag was not large and, if it only contained aspers, they would hardly make up a single lira. Then where would I find more money? Time was getting on. Oh, if only they were piasters! Finally, I could bear it no longer and plunged my hand into the bag. I saw the glint of gold in my palm. Liras! Not five, not ten . . . I looked round to make sure that no one was approaching, then counted them with shaking hands. Two hundred. Two hundred liras! Now I understood why my uncle had shouted after me in such alarm and despair.

Two hundred liras! Even if my brother and I managed to pay him back during his lifetime, he would never forgive us. I suddenly thought of Aunt Tanasa, Rainichka and Hinko, and realized that the money was theirs as well as his. What did I need two hundred liras for? A quarter of that amount would be enough for my venture. I felt somewhat uncomfortable and guilty. I felt like a thief for the first time. I looked at the fishermen out early with their boats, and listened to their steady singing, drifting over the waters, and I wondered what to do. I told myself that I would count out fifty liras and throw the rest over the wall into Hadji Doino's courtyard. But if someone else found the bag, would whoever found it give it to him? Or I might send somebody with it. No, anyone I gave it to would open it on the way and that would be the end of that. I racked my brains, hunting for a solution.

What a silly, childish idea! As if returning the money would stop Hadji Doino from threatening or pursuing me! He must have been to the police station already and told them about me and my brother and why I needed the money. So I might just as well keep it. It could be of use to someone. My brother was not the only prisoner going into exile.

The thought of the prisoners made me jump to my feet and set off towards the bridge. The *Osmanieh*—that was what I had to see first. Was it there? When was it due to leave?

The ship was still in the same place at the pier, and only the puffs of black smoke issuing from its two funnels indicated that it was ready for a long journey. The prisoners were nowhere in sight. It's early, I thought, with relief, and went over to the ticket office to buy a ticket.

"To Samsun? Four lira," said the surly ticket agent with a contemptuous look, as if wondering how a ragamuffin like me had come by so much money.

I paid, pocketed the ticket and started back towards the ship. I wondered whether I should go on board before they brought the prisoners. What if something happens, and they don't bring them after all? I had not bought any food for the journey, I had no overcoat, I was barefoot and in rags.

Going by the bridge I passed through a bazaar. I did not notice what they were selling, but I hoped that I would find what I needed. I started to hurry, and it was well that I did, for before I had left the waterfront, I saw an apparition on the pier that made my heart stand still. A short, fat man, with a broad face and a drooping mustache, was pacing angrily up and down, leaning on a stout walking-stick. Although I was too far away to hear him, I knew that he was choking and spluttering with rage. Beside him, a rifle over his shoulder, hobbled a bandy-legged zaptieh.

They were looking for me.

I hid behind some foul-smelling crates and kept a close watch on them. Hadji Doino hurried over to the ticket office, poked his head in at the window to ask the agent if he had sold a ticket to a boy answering to my description. At once he shouted something to the zaptieh and the two of them rushed up the gangplank onto the ship.

I do not know how another person would have felt in my place, but at that moment I hated my uncle so intensely that I did not even feel afraid. Something in me had changed. He knows why I am taking the money, I thought, yet he had to bring along a zaptieh to stop me. No, no! Hadji Doino is no uncle of mine now. He is no Bulgarian; he is in league with the Turks, an enemy. An upstanding man is not afraid of enemies; he fights them.

So I argued to myself, from my fourteen years of experience, as I crouched behind the pile of smelly crates and watched Hadji Doino and the policeman running back and forth on the *Osmanieh*.

Suddenly I thought, "How will I sneak onto the boat when sailing time comes?"

How? I hesitated only for a moment. I'll dress up as a Turk. Just as Levsky did! I had often heard them talk at home about the fearless Deacon Levsky.[1] Yes, of course, if I donned Turkish costume, Hadji Doino would not even glance at me.

No sooner said than done. Luckily for me, the bazaar by the bridge had everything I needed—a fez, a turban, a blue embroidered waistcoat, a belt, wide-bottomed breeches and yellow moccasins with turned-up pointed toes. I hid behind the booths of the second-hand clothes dealers and put on my new attire. Balyu watched me in wide-eyed amazement.

---

[1] Vasil Levsky (1827-1873), known as the Apostle of the Bulgarian Liberation, organized underground resistance against the Turks. He was eventually captured and executed.

"What is it? Don't you recognize me?" I laughed. He bared his teeth in reply, as if to say that he did not find my appearance to his liking.

"I am not too keen about it either," I said. "But it has to be done, or we'll never get on the ship."

He obviously understood, because he wagged his tail and, as usual, snuggled up to my legs.

This reminded me that Hadji Doino would still recognize me by my dog. So should I leave Balyu behind? No, not for anything in the world! Usually I would have been at a loss, perhaps even afraid. But something had happened to me that morning. Now I thought quickly and came to decisions fast. I soon found a way out. I bought a couple of sacks from the old-clothes dealer. I filled one of them with provisions for the journey and put Balyu in the other.

"If you bark, it will be the end of both of us," I warned him.

He lifted his head, nuzzled my cheek with his wet nose and stuck out his tongue.

"Come on, come on!" I said. "Don't fawn over me! Stay down and keep hidden."

I slung the two sacks over my shoulder and walked back towards the pier. I walked with a bold, confident stride, but my heart was in my boots and I was anxiously wondering, at the back of my mind, what would happen if Hadji Doino discovered me.

I was just leaving the bazaar when I saw a stand where they were selling mirrors of all shapes and sizes. It was mobbed with women, and there was not a man to be seen except the salesman, a Greek. Driven by curiosity over my new appearance, I went round and walked slowly past the stands. A large looking-glass with a bronze frame showed me a tall slender youth whose face looked strange yet oddly familiar.

Goodness, that was me!

I examined my reflection and could not believe my eyes. It was not the Turkish costume that took me by surprise, but my face, my expression, my bearing. What a change in those two months since the great upheaval in my life! I still regarded myself as a boy, but gazing back at me from the mirror was a young man, with strong features in a freckled, sunburnt face, his gray eyes intent and stern. I had grown up without realizing it. Hardship and danger had transformed me. Life is so arranged that no experience is wasted.

I set off cheerfully towards the pier. It was already thronged with departing passengers and people who had come to see them off. Hadji Doino and the policeman had taken up their stand, one on each side of the gangplank. I passed between them with my back turned to my uncle and my face to the Turk, walked up the plank (was it really swaying beneath my feet or were my legs unsteady?) and boarded the ship.

I was met by a bearded sailor with a bandanna on his head. He said something to me and, although I knew Turkish well, I was so taken aback that I did not understand a word. However, I took my ticket out of my belt and gave it to him. He grinned broadly as he took it, saying, "Hurry up and find a place for yourself. There's water on the foredeck."

I nodded and hurried off, wondering what the "foredeck" could be and what water he was talking about. I passed under a large awning, went up a gangway and found myself in a wide open space. At the far end by the two smoking funnels was a large pipe with a tap. A man was squatting in front of it and washing himself. Two others, kneeling on a worn mat, were stretching their arms heavenwards, dropping them, and then bending over till their noses touched the ground. They were praying . . . and the water . . . of course, why hadn't I thought of it? The water that the sailor had mentioned was for washing before prayers, according to Turkish custom. But how strange and how funny that he should have told me this! Here was the deck and here was the water. All I had to do was to wash, kneel down and pray like the others to Allah to give me a calm sea and a safe landing at Samsun. Why should I think it strange or funny? Hadn't the clothes made a Moslem out of me?

Down by the bridge, I saw that Hadji Doino was still on the lookout. Then my gaze shifted instantly to the unhappy band of prisoners, who were slowly approaching from the street across the way. The whole pier rang with the clanking of their chains. "Come on! Step lively!" barked the zaptiehs, walking beside them. Once again I heard the lashing whips and the oaths and curses which I had had to endure all the way from Plovdiv to Tsarigrad, and I just could not get used to because they seemed so unworthy of a human being.

I looked for Lukan. But it seemed that someone else, even more impatient than I, had already spotted him. Hadji Doino! I saw him charge at my brother, with a thunderous face and clenched fists. Although I was so high up, I could hear him shout, "Hey, my money! My money!"

One of the zaptiehs escorting the group, not realizing what the man was shouting about or whom he was waving his fists at, hit him so hard in the face that his scarlet fez rolled in the dust and he clutched his cheek with both hands, cringing like a beaten dog. Only his voice continued to whine and complain. Although I could no longer hear him, I was sure that he was saying, "Why do you hit me, aga? Hit *him!* His brother has robbed me and is trying to rescue him. The whole family are brigands . . . rebels."

Neither the policeman nor the prisoners paid any attention. One by one, linked by the chain, the prisoners boarded the ship and filed off towards the stern. Apparently the *Osmanieh* had only been waiting for them, because the sailors promptly raised the gangplank, the bell clanged, a deafening roar rent the skies, and the two funnels started belching clouds of black smoke. The *Osmanieh* swayed, then, drawn by a tiny tugboat, slowly glided away from the pier.

"All-merciful and glorious king of the seas, lord of the storms, ruler of man's destinies, vouchsafe us a calm journey and a safe landing," whispered the faithful kneeling beside me, and bowed their heads.

My eyes wandered to the after-deck below where, hemmed in by zaptiehs, my unfortunate compatriots were huddled together. Wasn't that Lukan over there with the reddish hair? I could not see his face but I was sure it was my brother. He was facing towards the slowly receding town, gazing at its crenellated walls, the towers of its palaces, the tapering minarets of its hundreds of mosques. It really was extraordi-

narily beautiful. Yet I knew that, at that painful moment, he was neither seeing it nor thinking about it. He must surely be remembering our far-off native land, our beloved town nestling among the forests and the mountains, and wondering perhaps if one day he would ever go back there, or if his bones would rot away in the wild wastes of Anatolia. At that moment he may also have been thinking about me, thinking that I was somewhere there on the shore, and that all my childish efforts had been in vain. Oh no! He must not think that; he must believe in me and not lose heart. I was there where he was, and no longer had any doubts—no other thought but to save him.

I opened the sack containing Balyu, helped him out, and showed him the after-deck.

"You see Lukan over there? Go up to him, so that he'll know."

Balyu looked at me, blinked, then wagged his tail and picked his way between the piles of baggage and the thick coils of rope. I soon lost sight of him. However, he knew his job.

A minute later I saw his sandy rump squeezing through the ranks of policemen blocking the way to the after-deck. The next minute Lukan turned round sharply. Balyu had accomplished his mission and now my brother was anxiously looking for me. I made a sign with my hand and he nodded to show that he had seen me. As he moved, the sun caught his unshaven face. I do not know if it was only my impression or if it was really the case, but, despite the considerable distance between us, I saw tears glistening for the second time in his stern eyes.

My eyes, too, filled with tears. I felt like weeping with distress, with joy as well as with pride . . .

Part II

The Fortress

Chapter 6

I Walk into a Trap of Black Silence

ALL THE TIME I WAS ON THE "OSMANIEH," AND often afterwards, I tried in vain to imagine what Diyarbakir was like. In my mind I conjured up all the evil and horrible sights I had seen during my short life, but still no picture emerged. The whole lacked detail, and the combined terrors of dungeons, fortresses, and gallows became a blur in my mind.

On the eighteenth day after leaving Samsun, the mail caravan I was travelling with straggled out of the grim defile of Ambar-su. Our journey that day had taken us the length of that steep mountain ravine. I saw spread out before me now a strange, I should say spectral, valley. It was all black, furrowed and intersected by dry gullies, but black none the less. My gaze strayed off into the blackness. There was not a village, nor a hut, to be seen.

"What a rotten dump!" I muttered to myself, horrified at the thought that I would have to cross and possibly even live in that dead and barren waste.

No, perhaps I was wrong. Somewhere in the distance

flowed a river, a large river, but barely visible as, gray and dull, it meandered between the black rocky banks. Still further away, the white cap of a snowy mountain peak shimmered like a mirage in the haze.

"There it is! Over there, that's the Black Amid!" cried some of the travelers, pointing ahead beyond the river right at the peak, or so I thought at the time.

Was it that peak with the glistening snow that they called the Black Amid? How could they possibly call it black when it was the only speck of white in that truly black desert? I looked in some perplexity at Selim Baba, the mailman. The old man winked at me with his good eye; the other was swollen and bloodshot and I tried not to look at it.

"That's it, Ali," he said, using the name I went by. "We've arrived, boy!"

"We've arrived?" In my surprise I forgot about the stutter I had affected so that no one would notice when I made mistakes in Turkish. "I thought I was going to Diyarbakir!"

"So you are." He grinned. "We Turks call it Diyarbakir, but the Kurds and Armenians in these parts call it the Black Amid. There it is, see? Between the river—that's the Tigris, but it also has another name, Shat they call it—and the great Mardin."

He pointed at the snowy peak again, no doubt to indicate that the name Mardin referred to it.

Then where was the Black Amid, where was Diyarbakir?

I gazed again and, believe me, however incredible it may seem, it was only then that I discerned the dim outline of a town along the hills on the other side of the river. Crenellated walls, turrets, minarets—an optical illusion! But it wasn't. Since the whole of the surrounding valley was covered with that black rock, which years later I discovered was called black basalt, the town must also have been built of it. I must admit that the closer we came, the harder I found it to take my eyes off it. Was this where we would be living? What a sinister place and what a sinister town!

Soon we were so close that I could make out quite clearly its outline. From where we stood—we were now below the level of the town—the black fortress stood out harsh and forbidding against the distant backdrop of the white mountain peak. With its sheer, seemingly unscalable walls, it struck terror into my heart and, viewing it from the outside, I could already imagine what it was like inside.

And I was not mistaken.

When, one hour later, our caravan crossed the river Tigris by caique* and climbed the steep slope to the fortress, I felt as if I was deliberately walking into a trap. That is the exact word for it—trap. Behind us the iron gate slowly creaked to. Ahead, the main road branched out into steep side streets, dark narrow alleys with dirty, evil-smelling puddles left over from the recent rains, although the summer sun was unbearably hot and the air shimmered in the heat from the stone roofs.

Few people were to be seen, most of them zaptiehs. Now and then one would see the flash of a white Kurdish veil in the shadows, a swathed woman would scuttle past like a frightened cat, children would splash through the stinking puddles; then once again there would be dead, blank silence all around.

I didn't even stop to think where we were going. Selim Baba was taking the caravan somewhere and I walked on, with my dog behind me. Like me, Balyu had fallen silent and would not run ahead or wag his tail. Occasionally his wise eyes would look up at me and he seemed to say, "It's terrible here, Rali. There are no floggings or hangings, but it is even more terrible than the bridge at Plovdiv with the corpses." Was it in Balyu's eyes that I read this, or was I thinking it to myself?

It makes no difference.

If I turned to the left, I saw a wall of black stone, with a thick iron-studded door. If I looked to the right, there loomed another black wall with a tightly closed iron-studded door. I wondered what lay behind them. And weren't those overhanging stone eaves in danger of falling on our heads? But what oppressed me most of all was the silence. If only one heard the sound of a voice, even a swear-word. But there was nothing. The street was silent and our footsteps were muffled. Instinctively we kept silent too.

Finally the caravan entered a square. Like everything else in that accursed town, even this was surrounded by high stone walls. Then I happened to glance at the opposite side and, slightly to the left, I saw to my surprise that one of the doors stood wide open. I could see a path leading up to a shady courtyard, with a green hedge and a fig tree whose leaves were outspread like the fingers of a hand. It was the first greenery that I had seen since coming to the fortress and I felt comforted and cheered by it.

"Come into the inn," called Selim Baba. Then, turning to me, he said, "This inn belongs to Abu Talib. Stay here; you won't find a better place in the whole of Diyarbakir."

* * *

In the middle of the following month the band of prisoners arrived. That morning, as usual, I was loitering not far from the main gate. When I saw the mounted zaptiehs enter, with the men herded together like cattle, I abandoned all caution, flew down the steep slope and with pounding heart gazed at the pathetic figures slowly approaching, with the chain over their shoulders. On the boat I had learnt to tell them apart, had even mentally assigned them names of my own invention, but now they were so dark and so dirty from the sun and the journey that they were reduced once again to a dismal, faceless column. My eyes, travelling down it, however, immediately picked out my brother.

Lukan turned his head and looked around. Yes, he was looking for me. When he saw me standing in the shadow of the overhanging houses, he nodded excitedly and his face lit up with a happy smile.

"At last!" I sighed to myself, shaking with emotion and triumph. "You see, Rali, now he trusts you! He believes you will carry out your promise," a voice inside me said. How it strengthens you to know that someone has faith in you! I felt a sense of great comfort, and he must have been comforted, too.

I set off after the convoy. I had to see where the men would be imprisoned. Having grown accustomed to the deathly silence of the town, I was not surprised that the townspeople showed not a spark of curiosity about the new arrivals. In the prison there were already hundreds of exiles of various nationalities, so why should they look at these?

Perhaps I was wrong. Sometimes I had the impression that faces appeared at the thick bars of the little high windows. Whose were they? Why did they pull back so quickly? I didn't know and I didn't want to know. I hated that dreadful town. Furthermore, I was without any identification papers. When I left Panagyurishte there had been no authorities, no konak; therefore, there was no one to issue them to me and without papers I would not be able to leave Diyarbakir. Best not to think about that. I would not leave the fortress without my brother, and, anyway, my papers would not have taken care of both of us.

Walking along I wondered, for the hundredth time since I had come to Diyarbakir, how I was going to set him free. As usual, I could find no answer to the question, but that didn't discourage me. I'll think of something, I kept saying to myself. Somehow this familiar silent conversation gave me hope just as the green leaves I had seen on my arrival in the courtyard of Abu Talib's inn, had cheered me up. On I walked after the convoy, looking round from time to time to see if Balyu was following me. But my dog needed no reminder. He was investigating the side streets, with occasional backward glances, sniffing the stones and preparing to relieve himself. Poor thing, he was just as tired as I was of the inactivity and solitude.

Perhaps it was because I had grown used to the town that it did not seem quite so grim that morning. We went from street to street, encountering veiled women, urchins who looked after us with watery eyes, and even an entire battalion of nizam.* They filed past silently, impassively, as if the heat had drained away all their energy. However strange and however terrible everything seemed here, one got used to it eventually. It merely became tedious.

The convoy halted briefly in the large square in front of the Mutesarrif's konak. A plump officer appeared, yelled something at the zaptiehs and shook his fist at them. All I heard was, "It has been a whole week!" Then he escorted them up the hill to the fort, which I knew by then housed the prison.

This building resembled the outer fortress in that it, too, was black. But it had neither embrasures nor towers nor cannons, and it was not so high. Its single arched doorway stood out in bold relief. It was approached by a wooden drawbridge that was raised at night. I had often slunk past in the evening to get a clear idea of the layout. No, there was no chance of escaping from there. Sharp spikes protruded along the top of the wall as far as the eye could see. Even if the poor fellow found a way to clamber up there, he would be impaled on those rusty points.

There were no houses in the vicinity of the prison wall. It was surrounded on all sides by a grassy moat. On the side nearest me ran something resembling a broad, winding road, although it was all rocky and stony. On market days the Armenians and Kurds from the nearby villages came here by camel with their meager wares. In fact, it was the local market of Diyarbakir. Apart from this, there were a few shops in the square in front of the Mutesarrif's office, which sold guns, flour and olives, and about a dozen stalls in the surrounding side streets where one could buy clothing and miscellaneous articles. That was all. Yet there was a Pasha living in this town! This was the center for all the neighboring Armenian and Kurdish communities.

I recall that when Lukan and the other prisoners crossed the wooden drawbridge over the moat and disappeared one by one through the black arched doorway, I stood for a long time in the marketplace staring vacantly at the impregnable prison walls. How long I actually stood there I have no idea, but it must have been a very long time because I was suddenly startled by the voice of one of the guards at the little bridge.

"Hey you! Move off!"

At first I did not understand why he was driving me away. Perhaps he was not even doing that. He may have been shouting simply out of habit; after all, that was his job. I was afraid that he might suspect my intentions, so I hurried away.

I had scarcely gone more than a few paces when another voice, a familiar elderly voice, made me turn around.

It was the owner of the inn where I was staying, Abu Talib, the Arab. I recognized him at first glance by his height.

The Arabs were not tall usually, but Abu Talib, the inn-keeper, was the tallest man I had ever seen. In addition, he was thin, scrawny. He was completely enveloped in a white sheet, over which he wore a black mantle. I thought he looked like a bird, perched there on his shiny brown legs.

"What are you doing here, son?" he asked, coming up and walking along beside me. I muttered something vague in my embarrassment.

He bent his head and eyed me inquiringly, I thought.

"I have never asked you, but why did you come to our town? Where are you from?"

I had already thought up replies to these questions some time ago. But now his words brought back the excitement I had felt a little while back when I had met my brother's eyes. A daring thought took shape in my mind. Could Abu Talib help me in some way? Nonsense! Be careful, Rali, watch out! I dismissed the dangerous thought, but it came back again. After all, Abu Talib was not a Turk but an Arab. Perhaps he did not like the Turks. Or supposing I gave him half my liras? I don't know . . . I don't know . . . I became thoroughly confused.

I heard myself saying the very thing I had sworn so often to conceal: "I came because of the prison, Abu Talib."

Before I had completed the sentence, I realized what I was saying, and fell silent. Apparently my silence was more eloquent than my words, because the Arab stopped, glanced round quickly, and asked in another tone of voice, "Is it your father?" He nodded in the direction of the prison. "What is he in there for?"

Now I had given the game away. But hadn't I done it deliberately? How could I retract now? He had asked if my father was there. Oh, well, father, brother—what difference did it make? It made no difference so long as he did not find out that I was a Bulgarian. I realized more clearly than ever

how careful I had to be. Like everyone else at the inn, Abu Talib knew me by the name of Ali. If I revealed that I was not a Moslem, he would call me a liar and never speak to me again. But now I am thinking about myself. What does it matter to me? It's my brother I should think of. The important thing is that I must not give him away. The tension and misery brought tears to my eyes.

"Don't, Ali. Don't cry, son." With unaccustomed tenderness Abu Talib laid a thin hand on my shoulder. "The will of Allah," he said soothingly and looked up at the blazing sky.

When he bent his head to me again, a change had come over his swarthy face with its bristly gray beard. I could not exactly define the change, but I felt it at once.

"Listen to what I have to say," he continued. "I, too, once had a son. I had one once but Allah decreed otherwise, and now I have none. He was hot-blooded, Ali, and he raised his hand against one of the notables of this town. I was living somewhere else at the time. And that was that. He was exiled to Akiya.[1] Do you know where that is? You don't know. Well, it's at the end of the world, son. He went away and never came back."

As Abu Talib was telling me this sad story, so like my own, the two of us kept walking along the sun-scorched road. I listened to his resigned voice, thinking that now there was no going back, that I would now have to tell him why I was here. I would have to invent and lie and, at the same time, admit that there was a close relative of mine in the prison whom I had come to see. "I can tell him anything just so long as I don't let him know that I am a Bulgarian," I repeated to myself, though it was quite unnecessary for me to repeat it. I had not given myself away at the beginning, so why should I now? Very well, I'll tell him that my father is there, I'll say his name is Osman. But why was he in prison? Why?

I thought of what to say just as the innkeeper finished his story—for exactly the same reason that his own son was punished! In that case he would be all the more inclined to be-

---
[1] Akiya in Palestine.

lieve me and all the more sympathetic. With much stuttering and occasional feigned hiccups, I spun a confused yarn about an episode that took place in some village not far from Constantinople. It involved beys,* simple peasants, Moslems, old feuds flaring up, talk of unpaid taxes, and whatever else came into my head. In the end somebody killed someone else and my father was blamed. Then the zaptiehs . . .

Abu Talib laid a restraining hand on my arm.

"Tell me no more," he said. "I can imagine the rest."

My words must have reminded him of some painful experience of his own, because he suddenly began to stride along at such a rapid pace that I could hardly keep up with him.

We were skirting the big Uluk mosque with its rectangular minaret, which had once been the steeple of an Armenian

church, and were very near the square in front of the Mutesarrif's office when Abu Talib suddenly said, "Were you able to see him?"

"No," I lied.

"That's what I thought. You came too late. Until a short while ago the local citizens could stand surety for a prisoner and take him to work for them at home."

"And now?"

He shrugged his narrow shoulders, his grizzled beard sinking between them. It was a more eloquent gesture than any words. Abu Talib then told me what had happened to change things.

"It is all because of the giaours,* son," he said. "Ever since they started bringing them here in droves, conditions have become bad for the Moslem prisoners. They are not allowed out alone any more. Whenever they are taken out to work, they are always on a chain. But Allah is good, don't be so downcast, Ali! Listen . . ."

As some mounted policemen were riding by—in that town zaptiehs were more frequently encountered than ordinary citizens—he stooped down so that he could whisper in my ear. In a low voice, he said, "I'll tell you how you can see your father."

"How, how?"

He smiled significantly and winked.

"Take a can of boza* and go and sell drinks to the guards."

"But they won't let me inside the prison, Abu Talib."

"They'll let you in, son. Sell at half price, and you'll be welcome anywhere—that is the way of the world."

Chapter 7

It Is Not Always Easy to Be a Boza-Seller

MY INSTINCT HAD BEEN RIGHT IN TELLING OLD ABU Talib my troubles, and he helped me.

About two weeks later, lugging a can of boza, I entered the prison unhindered, rattling my tin mugs and shouting at the top of my voice:

"Boza, tangy boza-a-a! Only one asper a mug! Lovely boza!"

I really was selling the boza cheaply. I lost two piasters on every can, which meant that since taking up this occupation I had lost half a lira. But who cared about money? The main thing was that the guards got used to me. The sergeant, a swarthy Kurd with protruding eyes and a whiskery face, grinned broadly whenever he saw me.

"Come on, boy, do hurry! This heat is turning me into pastrami!"* he cried and chuckled slyly, reaching for the mug.

I watched him drink noisily, blinking and grunting with satisfaction. Although I was horribly afraid of him and repelled by him, I gaily extolled my boza and invited him to have another mug.

"Ah, it's tasty, marvelous!" He smacked his lips and, as usual, pretended to forget to pay. Because of this his whole expression seemed to say: go ahead, I'm not stopping you. Enter!

That was just what I was waiting for. I quickly grabbed my can and went down into the prison yard.

Don't imagine that it was by chance that I said, "I went down into the yard," because, after passing through the arched gate in the wall, I suddenly found myself confronted by something resembling a gigantic well. It was a black abyss enclosed by black walls, into which one descended by means of countless worn, chipped steps. From below wafted a smell of urine and filth, and it was this stench that told the visitor where he was going and what awaited him inside.

The first time I went down to the dungeons, I felt as if I were entering a bottomless grave. In the semi-darkness my feet could hardly find the steps. I stumbled down blindly, thinking all the time that I would go hurtling to the bottom, to the source of the stench and that dull, ominous rumbling sound.

Was it voices, the echo of distant cries, or groans issuing from the very walls?

Balyu, his fur bristling with fear, walked beside me. On my other side wheezed Suavi Kütük, the Onbashi.* At times he would mumble; at others he would squeal like a pig.

"Go on, shout! What are you waiting for?" he ordered with a nervous titter, slapping me on the back as if in friendly jest. Twice this jest of his nearly sent me flying headlong into the abyss with my can and mug.

I started, "Boza-a-a! Nice . . . tangy . . ." but my voice was so faint from fear and excitement that it was barely audible.

I peered through the barred windows and doors which were dimly visible in the surrounding walls. There was dead silence. Narrow stone passages led to them from the steps. Occasionally a shadowy figure would be glimpsed, but in the darkness I could not see what it was. Only the gray gleam of a bayonet would tell me that it was a guard. Or a voice would call out, "Hey, boza-seller, come over here!"

I was ready to go wherever I was summoned, always hoping that I might find Lukan. Suavi Kütük had taken it into his head to drag me down to the bottom of the yard where—so he said—the demons lived. I had to go. I admit now that the Onbashi was right. It was living hell. He was wrong on only one point—the identity of the demons.

When I finally walked on level ground, I stopped, dazed for a moment. High above me shimmered the white-hot sky, closing down on us like a lid. Black walls surrounded me on all sides. In them yawned cavernous holes, with massive iron bars across the openings. From the fact that I could make out these iron bars and the entrances to the cells, I guessed that somewhere inside there must be a glimmer of light, although I could not actually see it. The air was fetid and so dank and chill that I was shivering.

"Go on, shout now!" ordered the Onbashi.

I opened my mouth to shout, but no sound came out.

"What's the matter! Have you swallowed your tongue?" demanded Suavi Kütük and squealed with mirth. "Scared, eh? Go on, shout! They'll come."

I called out, then again, louder. Perhaps somewhere in there my brother would hear me. Would he know it was me?

My voice rebounded from the walls, drifted up the steps and finally died away.

"Boza . . . Bozaaaah!! Only one asper a mug. Delicious, spicy," I shouted desperately.

Suddenly the surrounding walls seemed to come alive. I did not know whether there were cloisters inside or little rooms for the guards, but quite unexpectedly lanterns began to appear—one, two . . . four! The lights were swaying, coming nearer. I saw the ugly, stubbly faces of the guards coming towards us. But Balyu had seen them before I did and started to growl and bark. If I hadn't told him to keep quiet, he would very probably have leapt at their throats.

"Where are you, boza-seller?" I heard voices ask. "Pour some out. A cup of hot coffee would have been better, but since there isn't any, we'll have to drink boza."

Four guards stood around me, all with outstretched hands, anxious to be the first. Suavi Kütük tittered and squeaked.

That day I had brought only one mug and I deliberately took my time pouring the boza. As I handed the mug to one and, when he had drunk, I handed it to the next one, my eyes wandered to the grating close by, brightly lighted by the guards' lanterns.

I still shudder to think of the poor devils who, drawn by the sound of my voice, had dragged themselves to the bars. They looked terrible. Frightful! No, that is an inadequate word, but I cannot find a stronger adjective. Hands clutched at the iron bars; emaciated bearded faces pressed against them as if trying to squeeze through. Huge sunken eyes shone in the darkness. Bate! Bate! Where are you? I can't see you.

"Here you! What are you staring at? You're pouring it on the ground, can't you see?" the zaptiehs scolded me. In my excitement I had missed the mug.

"The boy has never seen infidels before," the Onbashi explained in my defense. "Look, look! Do you see that one over there with the white beard? He's been here for twenty years."

He snatched the can from my hand and pushed me towards one of the cells, shouting, "Go on, take a look at him! Go on! The Padishah will give him a medal for distinguished service."

I put down the can! They could do what they liked with it. I walked up to the grating in a daze. These were the ones who should be getting my boza, all I had to give. Instead, the zaptiehs were drinking it. That was why Suavi Kütük had brought me here—double torture for those wretched prisoners and for me. I frantically scanned the faces, scrutinized them one by one. I had my back to the light and the prisoners could not possibly have seen me, but I saw them.

There, that must be the one. Twenty years! He was a tall man, not very old, but with a white beard. He was clad only in a shirt. His eyes—I still remember them—looked at me with such contempt and suffering. I longed to tell him, "I'm not what you think I am."

Balyu was bounding up to him. Why was he whining and wagging his tail? The white-haired man put out his hand and stroked the dog. No, it was not he. It was another man who had put out his hand, that one there. Bate! Bate! I clapped my hand to my mouth. Just one sound and all would be lost. I bent down quickly and by pretending to pull back the dog, I was able to grasp my brother's hand. He gave my hand an answering squeeze.

"Here, what's going on? Have you seen enough of the infidels, boy?" called the Onbashi from behind me.

"Why don't you bring us some boza instead," the other guards said. "You'll have plenty of opportunity to see them."

That was a typical day. Some paid, some did not. The next day I was back again. Twice during trips I attempted to hand him a file, without success. Nevertheless I still kept going there. I knew that my presence gave him strength.

Then one day, as I was passing by the cell, I saw a hand squeeze through the bars and dip swiftly into my belt. It must be Lukan, I thought. He was trying to show me where I should put the file.

As soon as I was outside the prison, I took the file out of my shirt and stuck it in my belt at the side. I'd keep it there and go up to the bars, pretending to be just passing by. At the same time I could pour out some boza for one of the guards. I tried to push the file further down, so as to hide it, but my belt was twisted. I straightened it and, to my surprise, I saw a scrap of cloth fall out. I picked it up.

Before I had smoothed it out I knew what it was—a piece

of my brother's shirt. On it was this message written with an indelible pencil:

"Rali, there is no escape from the prison. Wait till they take us out to work. Get . . ." Here the writing was smudged and I could only make out the letters "nd——ood." Then further on: "Go and see the slave Meira at Feisal Bey's house. Take greetings from her husband Bai Nestor, make plans together. Take care of yourself, Rali. Your brother Lukan."

This strange message made me so happy that after I had read it to myself for the tenth time I also read it aloud to Balyu.

"Do you hear? This is from Lukan. Poor fellow, what a job he must have had, trying to catch a ray of light from the lantern while the zaptiehs . . . But what am I telling you all this for? I have things to do now, Balyu. First of all I must find out who this Feisal Bey is and where he lives. Then I must find Bai Nestor's wife. Who is Bai Nestor anyway? Meira—what a peculiar name! Maybe she's a Kurd. If so, how will I be able to talk to her? I know, I know, it's easy for you, Balyu. You understand every language."

When I returned to the inn, I casually asked Abu Talib whether someone called Feisal Bey lived in the town.

The old Arab raised his bushy eyebrows and gazed at me intently before he asked, "What do you want with Feisal Bey, Ali?"

I felt myself reddening. It was a good thing that the lantern was some distance away and that people were constantly in and out of the inn. The mail train from Samsun had just arrived.

As I had done before in similar circumstances when I was flustered, I stuttered and stammered while I thought up an answer. Abu Talib did not take his eyes off me for a second.

I said slowly, "I heard his name today. They were talking about him outside the Mutesarrif's office."

"Who was?"

"Well, there were two of them."

"Two of them?"

"I don't know who they were."

"So, what were they saying?"

By now I did not know what lie to tell. "Well . . . one of

them said that he was a good man. The other one shouted, 'No, he's bad.' "

"That's right," the innkeeper declared, then became thoughtful. "As a human being he is bad. They say he can kill without batting an eyelid. But apart from that, he is a good Moslem, my boy. You know the little mosque? Well, he built it. May Allah grant unto all men such deeds!"

I nodded, appearing to agree with him, but inwardly I felt a sudden hatred for Abu Talib. He himself was just like Feisal Bey. He was ready to call a murderer good, provided he had built a mosque to Allah. Yet when he talked about his own son . . . but perhaps not. I don't know. I became confused. I was up against something complex—something I could not understand. I should not be hasty in my judgements. Hadn't Abu Talib told me how to get into the prison? Didn't I always go to him for advice? If one of us was dissembling and lying, it was I, not he.

What then?

I simply felt that I could not trust him entirely.

A little later on that evening another conversation took place at the inn. It was quite different from the one I had with Abu Talib. It so affected me, coming on top of everything I had gone through during the day, that I tossed and turned all night long and could not get to sleep.

Selim Baba had brought a newspaper with the mail. The town clerk undertook to read it, but he took so long spelling out the words that the local citizens squatting around him finally lost patience. To lose patience in that town was something unusual.

That made me prick up my ears.

"Come on, tell us, Ibrahim," they clamored. "Why do you take so long?"

"Why don't you say something?"

They bombarded him with questions from all sides.

Ibrahim raised his head, sniffed with his long nose, and looked at each of them in turn.

"How far have our troops advanced?" put in Hadji Hassan, the oldest of them and one of the regular visitors at the inn. He secretly drank brandy and his face was always puffy.

"Well, Hadji, it's like this! Our troops, you can be sure, are about to enter the capital of the Serbian giaours. But there is something else, Hadji . . ." Ibrahim broke off, falling silent.

While the squatting men were racking their brains to guess what this other thing could be, I suddenly remembered the snatches of conversation I had overheard on the ship about some war that was being fought between the Ottoman Empire and the small principality of Serbia. This war had apparently started just after our uprising in Bulgaria and, like the uprising, seemed to be headed for a bad end.

Being taken up with my own problems, I had not given it a thought until then. I might not have thought of it even then, if I had not seen the bewilderment and fear in the town clerk's eyes.

He spoke finally. "It says here, agalar,* that the Russians have entered the scene. They are threatening war. That is to say, they are planning to fight us."

"Wait a minute—what do you mean, the Russians?" demanded Hadji Hassan, frowning.

His companions started yapping in chorus like excited curs:

"Those Russians had better not poke their noses too far, or . . ."

"Why do those people always pick on us? Why does it always have to be Turkey?"

"Let them, Mehmed. Let them pick on us. Allah knows his business."

"Well, they will have their hands full, all right. The whole of Islam will rise up to a man, in defense of the faith. Right, Abu Talib?"

They all turned to look at the innkeeper. The fact that they were Turks and he was an Arab made his answer especially important.

Abu Talib took a sip of coffee, fingered his beads and finally replied, "Russia is great, agalar. Don't you remember what we all said that day when the captain was here? It is terribly powerful, so I heard from my father and my father's father."

He shifted another two beads on his amber chaplet and picked up his coffee cup. For a moment his companions looked at one another in dismay. Meanwhile, huddled in my smoky little corner, I gloated but at the same time trembled for fear of betraying my joy.

"What is the matter with you? It looks as if you are afraid of the Muscovite," burst out one of the Turks.

To encourage the others, he let out a harsh derisive laugh. I was so excited that I did not even look to see who it was. My eyes, smarting from the tobacco smoke, were fastened on Abu Talib. What would he reply?

Abu Talib gave a weary cough, ran his fingers through his gray beard and said, "You, Timish, are a brave man, I know. But listen, son, bravery and wisdom are not the same thing. War, Timish, is a bad business. However many set out, only half of them will come back."

"He who dies for his faith goes straight to heaven, Abu Talib."

"That is true, I know," agreed the innkeeper. "Now I have a question to ask you. Do you know why Russia is always spoiling for war? You don't. Then let me tell you. Because, my son, the Russian Tsar is an infidel and has made up his mind to destroy the Moslem empire. That is why. Wait now, don't be in such a hurry! You will understand why I am telling you this. The Muscovite has decided to build up a state for those giaours, the Bulgarians, who had an uprising recently."

"But didn't we wipe them out? What happened?" someone asked.

"The whole prison in Diyarbakir is packed with them," put in another. "There is no end to the swine."

Without looking at either of them, the innkeeper continued in the same even tone, "They want to set up a state for them, agalar. Where will they get the land for those infidels? They will take it from the land of Islam. The news Ibrahim read from the paper about the Serbian war—isn't it the same thing? Tell us, Ibrahim, doesn't Russia want to expand the Serbian State too?"

The clerk solemnly wagged his long nose. "That's it. Both the Bulgarians and the Serbs, that is what it says in that accursed newspaper."

Nobody knew what the innkeeper was leading up to. We all waited while Abu Talib took his time.

In the sudden silence that had fallen, the only sound to be heard was the water boiling in the coffeepot. Somewhere on the floor above a door banged loudly and feet clattered down the stairs. There must have been a sudden draft because I felt cold.

"Well, if that is the case, war is the only solution for us," said the aged Hadji Hassan. But there was a hint of uncertainty, however, in his voice.

Abu Talib screwed up his eyes for a moment and when he opened them again there was a new expression on his face, half mocking and half sad. He obviously considered himself wiser than his companions, and now, thinking it over, I can see that he really was wiser.

"This is how I see it, Hadji Hassan," he began. "No doubt there are those who attend to these matters. For the Padishah —may Allah give him long life—certainly has plenty of advisers of his own. But if you want my opinion, this is how I see it: we should avoid war like the plague, agalar. That is what we should do. We only stand to lose by war, and we have nothing to gain. That is why I hate the Rayahs.* They will not keep quiet as they should, but must always be starting rebellions, always making trouble. And what is the result? Other powers step in to help. Some help the Greeks, some the Serbians, some the Bulgarians, and then need you wonder that there is nothing left of our former glory."

"You are right, Abu Talib."

"Those are true words."

Sigh upon sigh greeted the innkeeper's speech. There was even some muttering about the Islamic empire going to the dogs. But instead of rejoicing at their despondency and gloating over their discomfort, I suddenly felt anxious. Some lurking danger threatened me, and the name of that danger was Abu Talib. Why had I told him so much? How could I retract my story now? He would probably suspect the whole truth one day.

The conversation went on for a long time. Eventually the

Ottomans recovered their spirits. They made the clerk read, word for word, what the newspaper said; then they all decided that if there was going to be a war, nothing could prevent it.

Even Abu Talib agreed with that. As he was bidding them goodbye, I heard him say, "You and I, Hadji Hassan, are growing old, but if it is Allah's wish that we should fight the infidels, we'll go with the rest. Come, I bid you a good night. Let us hope that the next newspaper will tell us that it has all blown over."

I, too, said good-night and went upstairs, where I found the worn-out travelers already snoring manfully.

My bed was not far from Selim Baba's. He must have been a light sleeper, because he stirred as I went past.

"Ali, is that you?"

I made no reply. I was tired of always being called by that alien name. I lay down on my bed but could not throw off my excitement. "Rali," I kept saying to myself silently, as if to convince myself that I was still the same person, that nothing had changed. What memories of home my name brought back! My mother—goodness!—I suddenly saw her there in the darkness, plump, red-cheeked and brisk, with graying hair escaping from under her kerchief.

"Here, Rali!" she called. "Where have you been loitering all this time? Come home at once."

She meant to be scolding me, but her eyes were so kind and tender that anyone would think she was saying, "Off you go, my boy. Go and play. Now is the time to enjoy yourself."

Now here was my father, also outwardly stern, as if his word was law. "Well, Rali, why weren't you at school today? You had better watch your step—do you see the shop? It's waiting for you."

Oh mother, father—how sweet your voices sound to me now that you are gone! Here I am among strange, evil people, not daring even to tell my name, and look!—just the memory of you warms me, takes me back to my home, to our town and the old familiar world.

I remember that I lay there for a very long time, reliving those far-off days that had gone for ever. I grieved and cried to myself until, somewhere outside in the yard, a long drawn-out dismal howl shattered the silence. It was repeated a second and a third time, a dreadful piercing cry. I suddenly realized that it was my Balyu. Somehow I must have communicated my unhappiness to him. He, too, was pining for our old backyard, for the gaily bustling streets of our little home town, and for the fields and hills where he used to run wild.

Dear old friend, try and put up with it a little longer—for how long I don't know myself, but be patient. We'll find Bai Nestor's wife (I already felt as if Bai Nestor were an old acquaintance). We'll plan the escape then one day. "One day," I repeated, and already saw myself on that day, fleeing with Lukan through forests and over mountains, reaching Samsun. There was the ship *Osmanieh*. Then on to Tsarigrad, then Panagyurishte, with Balyu following us all the way. But it would be madness for us to go back to Panagyurishte, I reflected. It was madness, I knew. Nevertheless we would go back if only for a day, for an hour. Just to walk through it. Just to breathe its cool air, to see the ruins of the house where we had been so happy once.

The tears came flooding to my eyes. I turned over on one side, so that they would fall onto the mattress, because my hands were already wet.

Of a sudden I had a vivid recollection of the conversation that had taken place downstairs a little while ago. Russia was preparing for war. That stranger, that friend of Lukan's, had foreseen just this. She was preparing for war against the Ottoman Empire. She was going to fight for us. For us! To rid our country of the Turks for ever and set up a Bulgarian State of our own!

Suddenly I saw all my dreams of escaping with Lukan and walking through Panagyurishte in a new light. Like an unleashed torrent, like a herd of wild horses, thoughts raced through my head. I snatched first at one, then another, and basked in happy anticipation of what it would be like to be without masters, what it would be like to be free.

Chapter 8

Bai Nestor's Family

NEEDLESS TO SAY, THE NEXT MORNING I OVERSLEPT. When I woke up, I found that Selim Baba's party had left the room. I looked out of the little crooked window. The sun, dazzlingly bright as usual, was a whole span above the city walls and the flat black roofs of the houses glittered beneath its fierce rays.

I got up, put on my clothes and hurried downstairs.

Abu Talib was sitting cross-legged by the counter, where the morning's pilaf* was bubbling on a small stove. He had the tube of his hookah* between his teeth and was puffing at it rhythmically and intently.

The clatter of my hobnailed shoes made him look up.

"Ah, it's you!" he exclaimed, removing the mouthpiece from his lips.

I went up to him, made the traditional obeisance, and began, somewhat apologetically, "Somehow I had difficulty sleeping last night."

He nodded sympathetically. "Help yourself to pilaf."

I spooned some onto a plate and deliberately piled on more so that there would be enough left over for Balyu.

The innkeeper evidently guessed what was in my mind. "I have already given the leftovers to your dog," he said. "It seems you forgot to feed him last night."

Of course, in the excitement I had quite forgotten. Of course, that was why Balyu had been barking. I said nothing to Abu Talib, but inwardly I was grateful to him. Whatever he might have said in front of the agalar he had been kinder to me and my dog than anyone else in that town.

I finished up my pilaf, washed the can and mugs and prepared to set off.

"Are you going there, Ali?"

As always when he alluded to the prison, there was a note of compassion and fatherly solicitude in his voice. He had once told me that I resembled his son. Perhaps that was why he was so protective towards me. How differently he would have behaved if he had known that my name was Rali, that I was a giaour, a despised Rayah!

"First I am going to stop at old Assadurian's to buy some boza," I told him, "then . . ."

"Assadurian's you say? Wait, I have an idea. Weren't you asking me about Feisal Bey last night? His house is on your way. When you go out of the Armenian's shop and start up the hill towards the prison, you will see a high wall on your left. There is a large mulberry tree overlooking it. If the door in the wall is open, look inside, Ali. Look inside if you want to see a magnificent rich man's house, with carvings and niches. You could even sell some boza to the household. Say Abu Talib sent you, and they won't turn you away."

I nodded—without showing any interest, however—and walked out of the inn.

In the yard I was met by Balyu, who rubbed his head against my legs.

"I'm sorry." I patted him. "Forgive me, Balyu, it just so happened that I couldn't come last night. But I'll buy you a whole shoulder of mutton, I promise."

As I was whispering all this to him—for months he had been the only living being I could speak to in my own language

—we crossed the courtyard of the inn and came out into the little square.

The time I had spent in this town had taught me to look on it quite differently. Diyarbakir no longer filled me with terror, although nothing had changed since I had seen it the first time. I had simply grown used to the black stone of which the city walls, the houses and the mosques were built, and had learnt to recognize the inhabitants. Diyarbakir did not seem empty now. Soldiers' and policemen's uniforms still dominated the scene, but here and there it was enlivened by a brown Kurdish cloak, the cherry-red caftan* of an Armenian, the long white Arab shirts, reaching to the ground, and the brightly colored veils of the kadinas. Many of the Turks, particularly the soldiers, I already knew by sight. I had sold boza to some of them. They were not surprised to see me and would even stop and pass the time of day. I sometimes stopped them myself to make some casual inquiry, because no human being, by nature, can keep silent for long, even when he is among his enemies.

I filled up my boza can at Assadurian's, paid, then hurried off uphill towards the prison. I looked at all the doors I passed on the way. Which one could be Feisal Bey's? Abu Talib had said it was the most opulent-looking house. But from outside it was hard to tell which houses were opulent and which were not, because they were all hidden behind high walls.

"Boza-ah! Boza-ah!" I cried, stopping as if to look for customers, and trying to decide which house it could be.

Finally, I saw the mulberry tree that Abu Talib had mentioned. It certainly was an enormous tree, with its rustling branches spreading over the wall and its tired green foliage presenting a strange contrast to the glittering black walls all around.

I casually crossed the street, shouted "Bozadji!",* then went up to the door and gave it a push to see if it would open.

It was locked.

That was something I had not counted on. What should I do? Why, I'd knock! After all, Abu Talib had sent me, hadn't he?

I told Balyu to wait for me outside and I lifted the knocker.

Bang! Bang! the knocks rang out in the stillness of the morning. From the other side of the wall came a bark in answer. Behind me, Balyu began to growl.

"Shh! Keep still!" I cautioned him quietly.

It was just as well that I kept my voice low, because a minute later the iron-studded door creaked open and a face appeared round the crack. At first I could not make out whether it belonged to a man or a woman. It was a fleshy face, flabby and hairless, with little yellow eyes like a dog's. The hair was concealed by a multi-colored turban.

"What do you want?" The voice, high-pitched and unnatural, which, like the face, was neither masculine nor feminine, suggested that I was confronted with a eunuch.

"I was told to bring boza."

"Who sent you?"

"Abu Talib, the innkeeper."

The eunuch blinked, moistened his lips with a thick tongue and said, "All right, pour me a drop so that I can tell if it is good or not."

"It is good, aga." I called him "aga" to flatter him. At the same time I quickly filled the tin mug to the brim and handed it to him.

He drank the boza, smacked his lips and wiped them on his sleeve. "It will do. Come in, come in!"

I stepped into the garden, then stopped suddenly in surprise. From the outside I would never have imagined that this garden was so big. It was crossed by a network of little shady paths, all leading up to the house. They were overhung by vines, leafy fig trees, medlars and quinces, laden with fruit. Grass and flowers were everywhere. I stared. It was incredible. All this in Diyarbakir, growing on that black rock?

I felt a grudging respect for the owner of the house, thinking of all the soil he must have had to bring there, to lay down, cultivate and water.

"Come on! What are you stopping for?" said the eunuch. I followed him as he waddled on ahead, shouting, "Is anyone there? Fatima Kadin! Hey, Meira! Djidji Gugu!"

He continued to call out names and clap his hands, trying at the same time to ward off the large fierce dog which came bounding at us.

I quickly interrupted him. "Call Meira, aga. She is the one I was told to give the boza to."

"Meira? Very well. Hey, Bàba Meira! Come here, there's a boy to see you."

I was disconcerted by the fact that he called her "Bàba."* Could it be some other Meira? The letter said "Bai Nestor's wife." If I knew how old Bai Nestor was, I would have some idea of his wife's age too.

"I'm coming, Toparlak Bekir!" came a tired woman's voice although there was no sign of a woman in the garden.

"Wait here, she's coming," squeaked the eunuch and went off to take the dog away.

I stood and waited. Although I was preoccupied with the thought of the coming meeting, I still took the opportunity to examine the house Abu Talib had praised so enthusiastically.

Yes, he was right. It was magnificent.

Like all the houses in Diyarbakir it was built of stone. It was massive, almost as large as the Mutesarrif's building, and it obviously belonged to someone with money. Its two doors (evidently one led to the selamlik* and the other to the haremlik)* were decorated with stone carvings of flowers and interlaced designs, and had tiled porches. As in every Moslem home, the windows were protected by heavy bars. I was surprised at the large number of windows. They were ranged in a row, with unusual symmetry and harmony, and framed with borders of lighter-colored stone. There was something about them that looked familiar. Where had I seen windows like that before? I looked at the roof. Strange, very strange. On top it was flat, designed for sleeping out during hot summer nights; then slightly lower down it sloped outward, forming broad eaves. Although the eaves were made of tile, they reminded me so vividly of our wooden eaves at home in Panagyurishte that I could not take my eyes off them.

"Are you looking for me, boy?"

I turned round. A thin frail woman, wrapped in a faded shawl, had appeared from behind the house. Her face, which was partly uncovered, was gray and wrinkled, while her eyes, which were large and dark, hinted that she had once been young and perhaps even beautiful.

"Is your name Meira?"

She nodded.

"Abu Talib sent me."

"Abu Talib?"

I looked to make sure that the eunuch was nowhere near. He was still busy with the dog. "I'll risk it, whatever happens," I thought.

"Someone else sent me, too," I whispered. "Bai Nestor."

I saw her tremble. Her lips moved in an attempt to speak, then closed again.

"I have come on his instructions. But for the sake of appearances I am selling boza."

"I won't say a word," she whispered. "That means he is still alive. Thank you, O Lord!"

A Christian! I could not believe my ears. Her involuntary exclamation filled me with trust.

I quickly filled a mug with boza and handed it to her.

"Take this! Drink it so that the eunuch won't suspect anything. What did you call him just now?"

"We call him Toparlak Bekir."

She took the mug with trembling hands and lifted it to her lips, without taking her large dark eyes from my face.

"My brother is in prison with Bai Nestor," I whispered hurriedly. "I am not a Moslem. I am a Bulgarian, like your husband. In the letter from my brother, Bai Nestor asked me to find you. He wants to escape. He can't stand it any longer."

I had to break off. Muttering away in his squeaky voice, the eunuch appeared from beneath the branches of the quince tree. He apparently meant to come straight up to us, but a small flower bed blocked his path and he had to make a detour.

This gave the slave-woman a chance to whisper, "Come to the lower yard at sundown. There is a little door in the wall. I shall be waiting for you with Lilliah."

I did not understand. "With whom?"

But the eunuch was already too close to us and, instead of replying, she said out loud, "Your boza is very good. Sweet and spicy! Have you tried it, Toparlak Bekir?"

"I have, Meira. But if this young fellow will treat me to a mug, I shall have some more."

By now I was quite experienced in this sort of procedure and promptly poured him a mugful.

"We'll tell the master," said Meira. "Won't we, Toparlak Bekir? We'll tell him that the boza is good, just fine for the master's children. How much are you charging, young man?"

I mentioned a price, lower than that charged by the other boza-sellers, asked for a pitcher and poured some boza into it so that their bey could sample it too. Then I said goodbye, promising to come again the next day at the same time. But my eyes met the large weary eyes of the slave-woman and signaled, "Never mind about tomorrow. This evening I shall be at the appointed place."

Out in the street, where I found my faithful Balyu waiting in the shade of the opposite doorway, I suddenly thought, "Who can this Lilliah be?"

"Lilliah!" I repeated, puzzled and even rather annoyed. Contrary to my intentions and wishes, more and more new people were being let into the secret which, up to a month or two ago, had been mine and my brother's alone. First there was Hadji Doino, then Abu Talib, then Bai Nestor and his wife, and now this unknown Lilliah. Where would it all lead? Wasn't it foolish to confide in strangers?

While waiting for evening to come, I decided to let Lukan know that I had done his errand. I found a deserted spot, unfrequented by a living soul, took out a piece of paper and wrote:

"Bate, I went there and met M. This evening we will have a longer talk. Greetings to B.N. from his wife. Don't worry. I am here and have some money. I'll wait, as you said. You are always in my thoughts. Love from your brother Rali. Balyu sends his love too."

I was about to fold the piece of paper when I remembered that I had left out the most important thing. I hastily added, in large letters, underlined: "The Turkish papers say that Russia is going to make war on the Sultan. She is already mustering her troops. Hurrah! It's coming! Love again, Rali."

Half an hour later I was down in the dungeons. The guards greeted me like an old friend. By the grating where I expected to see my brother, however, there was only that fearsome gaunt man with the white beard, whom I had noticed on my very first visit. This time, too, he fixed me with his eyes but, strangely enough, they no longer frightened me. They had an appealing look in them. Could that be Bai Nestor?

"Look at him, Ali. Isn't he a beauty? Have a chat with the brute," sniggered the guards, no doubt drinking more boza than they intended to pay for, while my back was turned.

One of them added, "That's him, the bash-giaour.* Twenty years and still alive and kicking!" In trepidation, I went up to the prisoner. I wanted to ask him about my brother, but did I dare? Better to come back tomorrow. I'd shout louder, and I would bring Balyu along to bark. But what was that? I listened again. Someone was quietly, very quietly, whispering my name. "Rali! Rali!"

I strained my ears. The light from the lanterns barely reached his face, and his lips were hidden in the thick tangle of his beard. But his eyes spoke, and from them I realized that he was calling me. I was certain that he was Bai Nestor.

"Come closer," whispered the prisoner. "Your brother was feverish last night. No, he is not really sick. He'll get over it, don't worry. Did you go to Feisal Bey's house? How is my family?"

"Who are you?" I asked nervously.

"I am Nestor, Bai Nestor."

I quickly thrust my hand in my belt to take out the note for my brother. As always, the file was there too. I stealthily gave him the two objects and he concealed them in his hand.

"Well, what is the brute saying? What are you two talking about?" One of the zaptiehs came up and put a patronizing hand on my shoulder.

"He wants me to give him some boza, sir!"

"Boza, eh?" He roared with laughter. "We don't even give him bread, and now he wants boza. Those giaours are like gadflies! Go on, fellow, get away from there! Go back to your scoundrelly friends. So, they want to overthrow our empire, do they? All right, let them try!"

Bai Nestor made no reply. He backed away from the grating and slowly went inside to the dimly lit dungeon from which a faint, monotonous hum of sound could be heard.

There was nothing more for me to do there.

I collected three or four aspers for the boza. "We'll pay you the rest next time, Ali! Goodbye now, keep well." And I went out into the fresh air.

My happiness at last night's news and this morning's success had clouded over.

I thought to myself: "What can be the matter with Lukan? He had a fever, hardly surprising in that damp. I only hope he doesn't fall seriously ill."

I remembered that he had not even a jacket and that he probably slept on the bare stones. What could I do? How could I help him? And Bai Nestor too, poor man. Twenty years!

When I thought that I was only fourteen and that only a few months had passed since the uprising, those twenty years seemed an eternity. So Bai Nestor had already been imprisoned here before I was born.

And my brother was condemned to stay here forever, wasn't he? No, I would rescue him. We would escape at the first suitable opportunity and take Bai Nestor with us. His wife was a native of these parts. She knew everything and would help us. Lilliah would help us too. That must be Nestor's son. Or could it be Meira's brother? In the morning this mysterious, unseen Lilliah had frightened me, but now I suddenly visualized him as a powerful ally in the difficult task I had set myself.

I spent the rest of the day turning these thoughts over in my mind.

* * * *

In the south when the sun sets, dusk quickly follows. Only, in the fortress town of Diyarbakir complete darkness follows, rather than dusk, because of, apparently, the blackness of the walls on both sides of the streets. They were so high that they even hid the roofs of the houses, and not a glimmer of light could be seen. On a moonless night it was easy to lose one's way.

I did not wait until it was dark. Before the sun sank behind the city wall, I was already at the appointed place. As usual, Balyu was at my heels.

During the day I had taken careful note of the path leading uphill to the backyard of Feisal Bey's house. It was stony and exposed, but the long shadow of Dervish Mosque lay across it. Besides, with each passing minute the darkness was becoming more impenetrable.

Without pausing or looking round, so as to avoid attracting the attention of any chance passer-by, I quickly climbed the hill, found the little door in the wall, paused until I had caught my breath, whistled softly, then waited.

I thought I heard answering footsteps and the sound of whispering. But the door did not open.

I ventured a cautious knock.

"Who is it?" came Meira's voice from the other side of the wall.

"It is . . ." There was no use giving my name, as she did not know it. "The boza-seller is here," I said.

Did she recognize my voice? Evidently, because the door creaked open.

"Come in," Meira whispered.

I stepped in quickly. Balyu slipped in with me.

"What is that?" she asked in alarm.

"What? Oh, that's my dog. His name is Balyu. Don't be afraid, he won't bite you. What about your dog, where is he?"

"I tied him up. He is in the front garden." She bolted the little door and groped for my hand. "Follow me."

I set off behind her, or rather let her lead me. At the same time I tried to discover who was walking beside us, because there actually was a silent figure keeping pace with us. I could hear footsteps, and vaguely discern a silhouette in the darkness.

"Is that Lilliah?" I asked Meira in a whisper.

"Yes," she replied. Then, giving my hand a sharp warning squeeze, she said quickly, "Now be careful. We are passing Toparlak Bekir's quarters."

We skirted some huts. Two small windows, set some distance apart, were lighted. Further on was a third window and from this came a soft plaintive cry, like the whinnying of a horse. I listened and discovered that it was a tune. Toparlak Bekir was singing.

His song was very easy to remember. It went like this:

"Oooo...o...Eeee...e! Aaaa...ah...Aaaa...ay!"

And then again from the beginning:

"Oooo...o...Eeee...e!"

I could not grasp the significance of that series of vowel sounds and I only just managed to stifle a laugh, but Balyu responded with a bark.

"I only hope he doesn't notice that it is not our dog," moaned Meira. In the darkness I grabbed hold of Balyu and gave his ear a sharp tweak.

"You keep quiet!" I commanded.

He didn't make a sound after that, and the eunuch went on singing to himself.

"Now, quick!" said Meira, seizing my hand again. "Lilliah, run on ahead and open up."

We hurried past Toparlak Bekir's window and, without stopping, slipped in through the little low door which the invisible Lilliah had opened for us.

A minute later Meira bolted it from inside and we found ourselves in complete darkness.

➤ 101

"Let's hope your dog doesn't get into any mischief outside," said Meira anxiously.

"He's here, right at my feet."

This reassured her. Her voice was calm when she asked, "Can't you find the candle, Lilliah?"

"I'm lighting it now, mother."

I could not believe my ears.

A flickering light appeared at the far end of the low-ceilinged room, revealing a tall, slim, veiled figure. A hand reached out to straighten the candle, and it was the hand that convinced me that Lilliah was a woman.

Now, after all these years, I have to admit that the moment I saw her for the first time, I hated her from the depths of my being. So much for the help in which I had placed such high hopes. If that was where it was coming from, I felt like getting out and abandoning all of them—Meira and her Lilliah, and even Bai Nestor, whom my brother had so rashly (so it seemed to me) let into our secret.

My expression must have given my thoughts away, for the old slave-woman said, "Don't worry on her account, son—she is Nestor's daughter."

If Meira thought that she was reassuring me by saying this, she was mistaken. At that moment I was consumed with disappointment and childish rage. I had counted so much on that unknown Lilliah and in the end it had to turn out to be a woman. No, not even a woman, but a girl! From what I could see of her, she appeared to be my own age. What help can you expect from a fourteen- or fifteen-year-old girl?

I did not try to hide my annoyance. Although I had previously had a good opinion of Meira, I said, "If it's fear of betrayal you mean, then it's you I should worry about, since you are a Turk."

So you think the Circassians are Turks," she said, offended. "It is true that our people are Moslems too, but when I married Nestor I became a Christian. Lilliah is a Christian too," she added with sudden vehemence. "And what we have suffered from Feisal Bey on account of that, you have no idea!"

To convince me she pulled out a small metal cross from

under her mantle, held it up to my face and would not put it away until I nodded to show that I believed her.

"And what is your name?" asked Lilliah. "What are we to call you?"

Her voice was as musical as a bell, and rose and fell like the song of a bird. I like to hear voices like that.

"I'm called Rali."

"Rali! That's a nice name, isn't it, Lilliah?"

"Very nice, mother."

"There is a mat over there in the corner. Sit down, son," Meira urged. "We have nothing to offer you, Rali. The two of us are as poor as church mice—we are slaves—but the Lord will reward you for your kindness."

I sat down on the matting and the two women settled down, side by side, not far away.

The tallow candle was placed at the end of a little shelf. From time to time its flickering light fell on the faces of mother and daughter. How different they were and yet how alike! The mother aging, worn out by toil, and obviously ill. The daughter was as fresh as a rosebud, a little fragile but alert and eager. Her face reminded me in a way of Bai Nestor's. Her large eyes, nut-brown, slightly elongated and shaded by long lashes, were the Circassian eyes of her mother.

I told them briefly why I was in Diyarbakir and how I had met Bai Nestor in the prison. Nor did I forget to mention that I had seen him again that day. As they listened, the tears ran down their cheeks.

"There is just one thing I don't understand," I said. "How could a prisoner have managed to get married, unless he ran away and hid?"

Meira wiped her eyes and heaved a great sigh. "It happened, son, it came about. Even a slave in chains is still a human being. But the unhappiness, the suffering that followed . . ."

She fell silent, lost in memories. Now, remembering her sunken cheeks and lined face, I thought to myself: what a strange thing a human being is! Throw him into a dungeon, put him in irons, make him a slave, the lowliest and most abject of creatures, and still he is a human being, in fact, even more so than the rest. He still desires and suffers, still loves and grieves. Ah, we are all people, but it seems that we must each live through misfortune to realize that we are all the same.

Suddenly the old slave-woman gave a shudder, put an arm round her daughter's shoulders and looked at me, although I doubt if she really saw me. Her weary eyes had become remote and dreamy. Little specks of light danced in them, and her face seemed almost to grow young again. Then in rapid confused sentences, sometimes digressing and sometimes forgetting to explain a point, she told me the sad story of her meeting with the Bulgarian exile, Bai Nestor, and of their even sadder life.

I was so carried away that I could almost see them there in the hut before me, the young slave Meira and the young prisoner Nestor. Seventeen, no, eighteen years ago!

He had been sentenced to chains for rebel activities. I wondered what group he had been with and mentally enumerated the various brigades and uprisings that I had heard mentioned at home. Soon after his imprisonment, the local notables found out that he was a master builder. There was a general scarcity of builders, so they had him brought out of prison, his chains taken off, and set to work for them. When he built the city bath house, everyone saw how talented he was, and from then on there was keen competition for his services. After all, he was an exile, and would work for no more than a hunk of bread!

Feisal Bey was not slow to come forward. He took the prisoner, although everyone knew that he cordially detested infidels, set him to building some stables, then the little mosque, and finally his new house. That was why I had noticed something Bulgarian about it, I thought, remembering the neat arrangement of the windows and the eaves. It was there that Nestor had first met his slave-girl, Meira. It was there that the two had fallen in love. What could a rebel sentenced to perpetual banishment, and a girl sold into perpetual slavery do about their love? They were bold and they were desperate. They decided that they must get married, come what may! And they were married secretly in the Armenian church. Meira adopted his faith.

But has there ever been a perfectly kept secret?

When, a year later, the slave-girl gave birth to a child, evil tongues immediately began to wag and, of course, the first to discover the identity of the child's father was Feisal Bey.

He stormed and raged, thrashed and threatened. He wanted to kill Meira and throw the infant into the Tigris River. Then he reflected that he had paid as much as ten liras for his slave, had acquired a new recruit as well, and he finally calmed down. But he never forgave the infidel, Nestor. The bey drove him from the house and threw him back into prison. The rare occasions over the years when some other notable requested Nestor's services, were like rays of sunlight out of a dark sky for Meira and her growing daughter. Each time Feisal set to work and would leave no stone unturned until he had seen the offender returned to prison.

"So the years go by," sighed Meira in conclusion. "At first I had only one care in life, only one sorrow, and that was my husband. Now I have to worry about Lilliah as well. She is a big girl, almost sixteen, God bless her. And she's beautiful, but beauty brings no happiness to a slave, son. It brings nothing but trouble."

"Everything will turn out all right, you'll see!" I cried,

putting out a hand to comfort her. "We'll run away—all five of us!"

She shook her head forlornly. "How can we run away, Rali? We need horses, camels . . ."

"I'll buy them!"

"What about money? Do you know how much it would . . ."

I didn't let her finish. "Don't worry about money. I have enough!"

The women said nothing, but I had the feeling that they did not believe me.

"Here, you see!" I exclaimed, taking out Hadji Doino's leather pouch. "There are more than a hundred and eighty liras here!"

The gold glittered in my hands and it also seemed to sparkle in their eyes. Now everything looked different to them. They both began happily talking at once about what we were to do, what to buy, how much to pay and where to find it. We were so engrossed in plans for our escape that we did not notice how quickly the night slipped away.

"Goodness! It is time I was going," I said at last, jumping to my feet.

They sighed. It certainly *was* time. They saw me to the street and when, bidding them goodbye, I bent to kiss Meira's hand, she gave me a motherly hug and said in a husky voice, "Come again, Rali. All our hopes are in you, son."

Chapter 9

Abu Talib Drops Another Hint

FROM THAT DAY ON, I HAD REAL FRIENDS IN THE fortress town of Diyarbakir. At the same time my responsibilities had increased twofold.

In the days before crossing the Bosphorus, I had only my brother to worry about. For him I had stolen the money, for him I had exposed myself to danger and humiliation, for him I had plotted day and night how we should escape and where we should go. Now there was the additional problem of Bai Nestor, his wife and Lilliah. I was no longer disappointed that Lilliah had turned out to be a girl. Nor did I reproach myself for having given them hope, for their plight was so wretched that I could not forget it even if I had wanted to.

Consequently, one day sometime in the near future, the five of us would break away from the fortress and set off on a long journey. For that journey we needed horses, food, clothing and firearms. The supplies could not all be purchased at once, since that would attract attention.

From Abu Talib I rented the small hut which stood in the

courtyard of his inn and where he kept discarded odds and ends. There I began to lay in a stock of flour, cartridges, Kurdish costumes and waterskins. I do not know if the Hadji observed my sudden eagerness to acquire provisions in such quantity, but if he noticed, out of sympathy and understanding, he made no comment. Thus, by the end of autumn, I managed to buy two more revolvers and a carbine. I procured some dried meat, sugar loaves, tobacco for my brother, a small axe and knives, and more cartridges. Apart from the horses, which I wanted to buy the day before our flight, I now had practically everything ready.

The two slaves were also making their preparations. Only one thing remained—the most important of all—the escape itself.

Autumn passed, the cold winter months set in, and the fate of the prisoners showed no signs of changing. My brother recovered, fell ill again, and again recovered. I continued to visit the dungeon. As it was no longer the season for boza, I sold salep.*

"Salep! Salep!" I cried, as I had heard them do in my hometown. "Warms the gullet, cures sore throats! Salep!"

Of course, my salep was not for the sore throats of the prisoners, but for the guards and for Suavi Kütük, the Onbashi. All the same, I had good reason to bless the stupidity and greed of those trusting Turks, for I was able to pass notes to my brother on more than one occasion. I even managed to hand him a fur-lined vest through the grating, and a week later I took Bai Nestor a camel's-wool shirt that his wife had made for him.

Meanwhile, momentous and fateful events were in the offing. The news brought to us each month by Selim Baba's mail caravan caused more and more of a stir in the town.

How dead things had been in the beginning, when I had first set foot in Diyarbakir, and what a tremendous change I found by the end of the winter!

One would have said that the place was now inhabited by an entirely different population. Everywhere I went in the taverns, at the coffeehouses, outside the mosques and the

108 ◀

Mutesarrif's office, I saw chattering groups of men and I spent a whole day mingling with them in order to listen in on their excited conversations.

All they could speak of was the approaching war.

One day outside the Mutesarrif's office, I heard Hadji Hassan addressing a group: "So they said that they were holding negotiations at Constantinople. Some negotiations! They have broken them off. And who broke them off? The Muscovite infidel, the Tsar. He walked out."

"Let him go to hell, Hadji," growled a malevolent voice.

"Yes, let him go! But what happened then? Did they beg him to come back?"

His audience waited tensely.

"Who do you mean?"

"Our good-for-nothings!"

I listened in a state of exultation. It was the first time in my life that I had seen Ottomans so confused and afraid.

Old Hadji Hassan, who had obviously heard the news from the town clerk, although he spoke as if he had read it himself in the Constantinople newspapers, wrinkled his blue nose, knit his brows and launched on an explanation. According to him, it was the Ingilizler* who were to blame for everything.

"They are knocking on two doors at once," he concluded. "They want to have their cake and eat it too!"

One of the older listeners disagreed with him. "The English are on our side," he declared. "What you are giving us is politics, Hadji! Remember what happened twenty-five years ago when the Siege of Sebastopol began? Did the English abandon us then? Well, they won't abandon us now!"

"Allah alone knows, agalar," said Hadji Hassan with a shrug of resignation.

It was too cold to sit out there any longer, so they moved to the coffeehouse nearby, and I followed them in.

There they found the town clerk surrounded by another group of anxious Turks. As we came in, Ibrahim finished reading, put down the newspaper, and wagged his nose from side to side. We joined the circle.

"What's up, Ibrahim? What does it say?"

He regarded us all in his usual melancholy manner and said, "The Russian Tsar has ordered out the reserves."

"Is that so? Well, our reserves are being called up too."

"Let's hope for their sake that we don't strike first, or they'll be in for it," snapped a callow young policeman.

Suddenly the coffeehouse rang with shouts. What was the Padishah waiting for? Why did he not unfurl the holy banner? He had only to say the word and they would all come running to a man!

"But not everyone can go. We need people here too. Who will guard the fortress if the Muscovites—Allah forbid!—should surround it or if, in the confusion, our Armenians and Kurds should revolt?"

These words had a disturbing effect on the group, not only because they hinted at a danger to their homes and property, but also because they had been spoken by Feisal Bey.

I knew Feisal Bey quite well by sight now. He had recently become a frequent visitor to our inn and, as I looked at him, I would involuntarily compare him with Abu Talib. He was the same age as the latter, that is, approaching sixty, but he was short, stocky and broad-shouldered, with a thick, glistening beard. Unlike the Arab, he dressed ostentatiously, spoke loudly and set store by his position among the other leaders of Diyarbakir society. Even before meeting him, I already hated him for all the harm he had done to Bai Nestor's family. I not only hated him but feared him. Hearing him now, I suddenly realized that like many of the other townsmen he did not want to go to war. I remember Meira telling me that Feisal Bey had threatened to kill both her and her daughter but had finally desisted, not out of pity but because he would lose two slaves. So why should he have to go to war? Would he stand to gain anything? So long as there was nothing to gain, he would stay at home to guard the fortress, in other words, to guard his property and his goods.

As I said, Feisal Bey's words disturbed all his hearers. In a few days, as if his words had grown wings, they were buzzing through the entire town. Those very same words may well have been the cause of what happened a week later.

Late one afternoon at the beginning of March, already

springtime in Diyarbakir, Abu Talib took me out onto the roof of the inn. It was still too cold to sleep out of doors, so he obviously had something to tell me, something that the men downstairs were not supposed to hear.

He stood for a while in silence, leaning against the parapet, then suddenly raised his arm and pointed to the eastern wall of the town. The evening sun suffused it with a crimson glow, and the battlements and the towers with their copper cannons shimmered in a blood-red haze.

"Start counting from the Urum Gate at the south end," he said to me finally. "How many towers are there? One, two, three. Between there and the Mardin Gate there are twenty-five, right?"

"Yes, sir, twenty-five." I was very surprised and could only look from the city wall to Abu Talib's face and back.

He pretended not to notice my surprise.

"Have you been there?" he asked.

"Where, to the wall? Yes I have. Why do you ask, dear Abu Talib?"

"Did you see the state it is in, all crumbling and dilapidated," he persisted.

I mumbled something vague. I'd noticed, but I'd no reason to think about it.

"In a month's time it will be all fixed, Ali. Tomorrow they will start work. Over there by the Armenian graves, which you have probably seen, they will pull down the entire wall and rebuild it."

"Is that because there is going to be a war?"

He nodded.

I felt that at heart he did not approve of this war. The more excited the others grew about it, the more silent he became. Then why had he started this conversation? Or—at this my heart began to pound—perhaps he was trying to give me a hint of some kind.

"Abu Talib," this time emotion made my stammer quite genuine, "Abu Talib, do you suppose . . . do you mean to tell me that the prisoners . . ."

He nodded again, without looking in my direction. The last rays of the setting sun shone on his black mantle, but his face remained in the shadow.

Suddenly, from the minaret of the great Uluk mosque came the muezzin's cry: "Faithful! Faithful! There is no God but Allah, and Mohammed is his prophet! Death to the enemies of the true God! Death to the giaours!"

"We must go," said the old Arab, with a start.

"Where?"

"Down. Didn't you hear? It is time for prayer, Ali."

On our way down the stairs he stopped, waited for me to catch up and, although there was not a soul in sight, he whispered with a smile, "Do you suppose that old Abu Talib doesn't realize why you are hoarding all those things in the hut?"

I started to say something, but he laid a hand on my shoulder, telling me to keep silent. "I understand, Ali, and I love you for it. You are a good son. So, his time has come. Let Allah be my judge, but I shall never let a Moslem stay in prison with infidels, especially when our faith is in danger and we must all defend it."

"Abu Talib," I began unhappily. How complicated everything was, how difficult and dangerous it had all become!

"Don't worry, Ali, old Abu Talib knows whom to help and how."

One day, two days, a whole week went by and the prisoners never moved from their dungeon.

Abu Talib tried to reassure me. "There is nothing new about this, Ali. Why should you be surprised? Just be patient, my son, the time will come. I know from a reliable source."

I nodded to show that I understood, but I had lost heart. Surely all hope was simply a delusion.

During the week the excitement in the town rose to such a pitch that even at night people were to be seen in the street. Absorbed by my problems, I paid no attention at first to this unusual occurrence. I soon realized, however, that most of them were not local people. They were the reservists of whom Feisal Bey and the other elders had spoken.

After clothes had been issued to them and they had been trained, they would be sent north to the Caucasian border, or even to the Danube.

Yet the generally tense atmosphere did not affect me as much as it might have if I had not been completely occupied with my own affairs. Two or three times a day I would go to the eastern wall of the fortress to see if the prisoners had been brought out to work. I would wander around the marketplace and in the evening, I would steal away to visit Meira and Lilliah. They were no less excited than I was, particularly the mother. Her first words on seeing me would invariably be, "Have they brought them out?" "They will," I would reply confidently and repeat the words that the innkeeper had used to reassure me.

I gave the two women some liras so that they, too, could buy the provisions they needed for the journey. And I asked Abu Talib to buy me three horses.

"Why do you need three?" he asked in some surprise.

I needed five, not three, but I couldn't tell him that.

"The third one will carry the food and the waterskins," I quickly explained, for I had been prepared for just such questions. "Then one of the horses may be injured, or break a leg."

"That was sensible of you, very sensible," Abu Talib commended me. "As they say, 'he is a wise man who looks ahead and foresees everything.'" After those words of praise, he went off to the market, as it was market day and the Kurds from the neighboring villages were sure to bring horses to sell.

I took my pitcher of boza—now that spring had come, salep was no longer suitable—and set out with Balyu in the direction of the city wall.

I walked at a leisurely pace, secretly thinking that this would prolong the expectation and, consequently, my hopes. Perhaps I would see the prisoners today. I wanted to believe that I would see them, but the many months that had already passed had made me skeptical and resigned. If not today, then tomorrow. They will bring them out eventually, I told myself. We were going to escape one day. In that my belief was unshakable.

In spite of the early hour, the steep streets of the town were bustling as usual. I came upon the reservists struggling with heavy wooden chests and carrying gleaming guns on their shoulders. Long trains of camels straggled by, blocking the road. The streets rang with the clatter of horses' hoofs. The sound of shouts, curses, laughter and weeping mingled with the strains of the song which echoed from the surrounding walls:

There are none stronger than us,
None more glorious than us!
The crescent flag flies proudly
Over the bodies of the infidels!

For days on end they had been singing that refrain all over the town. It made me shudder. What could be happening at home now? Scenes from the uprising came to my mind: Bulgarians hacked to death, impaled, hanging and mutilated, villages burning, towns burning.

Without realizing it, I had reached the wall. At first I was so taken aback upon seeing the crowd of men, gathered at its base, that I was not even cheered by the sight. I stood rooted to the spot and stared at them. It was they! Some prisoners were on top of the wall, tearing at it with picks, hammers and iron bars. Others, on the ground, were lifting the heavy blocks of stone and piling them in huge heaps. The guards kept watch from the nearest tower and at the entrances to the nearby streets. Their long rifles shone in the morning sunlight.

I also noticed other guards patrolling up and down among the prisoners and flourishing whips at those who stopped to rest. Two by two, they went back and forth, dragging the stones, piling them on the heaps and returning for more. The muezzins had not yet called the second prayer of the day; yet in places the wall was already half demolished. If the prisoners continued to work at the same pace, by evening they would have torn down the entire stretch of wall between the two nearest towers. Once it was torn down—I had already outlined a plan in my mind—we would escape through the gap.

Suddenly, an anxious thought entered my feverish excitement. Had *all* the prisoners been brought out to work? Were my brother and Bai Nestor there?

I snatched up my pitcher and dashed off to look for them. "Hey, there! Where are you going?" shouted a voice behind me. Another voice thundered, "Stay away, boy, can't you see there are giaours here?"

"What, can't I sell boza to the giaours?" I called with my most innocent smile. "Don't infidels drink boza?"

The guards exchanged glances, without smiling. Although they shrugged their shoulders, they would probably have turned me back there and then if Suavi Kütük, the Onbashi, had not suddenly appeared.

"He is our boy," he said protectively. "He's allowed in. Go ahead, Ali."

I set off, but not before taking the precaution of offering him a free mug of boza, just for remembrance, as they say.

I walked among the prisoners, with Balyu trotting ahead of me. He, I knew, would lead me to the right spot and find the one I was looking for.

"Bozaaa! Nice tangy boza!" I yelled as loud as I could. "Two aspers a cup. If you try it you'll come back for more."

"Bozadji," called a wretched prisoner, whose cracked lips showed that he must surely have had a fever. "I'll give you my jacket for a mug. Will that do?"

It was like a slap in the face. Stop, Rali, can't you hear? Indeed I heard, but I also knew what would happen if I stopped, so I pretended not to notice him and walked on. When I had made the round I turned to have another look at him. The poor creature could hardly stand on his feet, and those beasts made him haul stones. Beside him walked another prisoner, a small man with a scar on his face, his eyes staring vacantly into the distance. The chain connected the left foot of one prisoner to the right foot of the other, so that neither could move without his companion. I was worried by this chain. It alarmed me.

I looked around at the other prisoners. They, too, were chained in pairs, and I now realized what was causing the continual jangling sound that filled the air and seemed to be all the sounds fused into one.

"Balyu," I ordered in a barely audible whisper, "quick, Balyu, find him!"

Supposing my brother was not chained to Bai Nestor! The thought that we might have to take two strangers along with us threw me into a panic. Never mind about the horses. As it was, they would not be enough for the five of us. And where would we find food for so many people, to say nothing of clothing, and weapons?

I followed Balyu, making my way among the little clusters of suffering humanity. In my imagination I was transported to some wild mountain gorge, like the one at Ambar-su, through which I'd journeyed with Selim Baba's caravan. There I saw the five of us, with the pair of strangers who had to join us because of the shared chains. We were struggling upwards, weak from hunger and thirst. We put our last ounce of energy into the climb. Behind us came a pack of pursuers, shouting and firing at us.

"They've caught us! They've caught us!" I heard myself mutter, and the sudden realization that I was speaking in Bulgarian startled me out of my reverie.

But there was no danger that the guards might hear me, had I been shouting at the top of my voice. I had wandered so close to the wall that the tearing down of the stone blocks drowned out all other sounds. Clouds of black dust hung over us. It got in the eyes, stuck to the perspiring faces of the prisoners. If I had found my two here, I should have had difficulty in recognizing them.

Balyu relied less on his eyes than on his nose. He suddenly began to whine. Wagging his tail for joy, he looked up at me with his intelligent eyes, then rushed towards a pair of dust-blackened men who were painfully dragging a huge block of stone as black as themselves. Hearing a dog bark beside him, one of the men turned around. That movement and the excitement written on the grimy face, told me that he was my brother.

The other was Bai Nestor.

Chapter 10

The Final Preparations

THERE IS NO NEED TO DESCRIBE IN DETAIL WHAT ruse I employed to approach my brother and Nestor, how I told them to be ready in two days' time and that I had made all the preparations. I supposed that if not that day, at least the next, Abu Talib would buy the horses.

My brother asked me to get a map of Turkey and a compass.

Bai Nestor merely whispered, "The day after tomorrow put a dried yellow mushroom in the boza and take it to the men up in the tower."

"What sort of mushroom? Why?"

One of the zaptiehs came up to us, so he could not reply.

"Well, I hope you didn't give any boza to that pig," said the Turk suspiciously.

"To him? What an idea? As if my boza were for infidels! Won't you have a drink, aga? Only one asper a mug."

The price of my boza went up or down according to the principle: the bigger the stick, the further the dog runs.

He had a drink. Then, having nothing further to detain

me there, I set off for Feisal Bey's mansion in the hope of catching sight of the old Circassian or her daughter. I had to tell them the news. They were just as impatient as I was. At the entrance I met the bey.

"What do you want?" he asked gruffly, evidently in a bad temper.

"The boza, bey effendi. I am supposed to bring it every day for the young masters."

He gestured towards the house and strutted off down the road. His gait betrayed his annoyance more than his face. Had he discovered that the prisoners had been let out? He had an old enemy among them, and the name of that enemy was Nestor, the master builder, who had built his house and the mosque he was so proud of, but dared to lay hands on one of the bey's own slaves. To Feisal Bey that was an unforgivable offense, the worst of crimes.

In the garden, as usual, I was met by Toparlak Bekir.

"Ah, it's you, Ali! Just a minute!" And he called out the names of the slaves in turn: "Come on, Djidji Gugu, Fatima Kadin, Meira! Come and get your boza. Mind you put on your yashmaks, now I see this boy is sprouting a mustache."

Hearing that I was there, Bai Nestor's wife hurried and arrived before the others, closely followed by the veiled Lilliah who, however, stayed by the door leading to the haremlik. She started a conversation with the eunuch, evidently in order to distract his attention.

"Pour me some," said Meira loudly, holding out the little earthenware pitcher that I knew so well by now. "What is it?" she whispered, although she had guessed the news from my face. "They are there? They're working on the wall!"

I nodded.

I saw her blink, rigid with emotion. "Thank you, O Lord!" she murmured. "At last you have heard my prayers."

I glanced at Toparlak Bekir. He was still talking to Lilliah.

"We are leaving the day after tomorrow," I told her, whispering. "I'll come over tonight and we'll settle the details. Leave the side door open."

"What about the horses?"

"I've made all the arrangements."

The pitcher was now full and she lifted it onto her shoulder, but still lingered. "Did you see him there?" she asked.

"Yes, I saw him and we talked. They are ready. They also have the file with them." Something in the expression on her face made me ask, "Why? Do you want to see him? It's dangerous. Besides, you couldn't get close enough to recognize him. He's all grimy from the dust."

She paused, trying to make up her mind. But I could not stay there any longer, for Toparlak Bekir was looking in our direction. So I called out to him, "Say, aren't you going to pay me for this week's boza?"

"I will, I will, Ali," squeaked the eunuch, promptly leaving Lilliah. "Tomorrow! The bey is out now and there is no one to give me the money."

"All right, then, tomorrow! Only don't say the bey is out again."

I took the empty can and made for the gate, but for some reason the last glance I exchanged with Meira left me feeling puzzled. She had obviously come to some decision. I could sense it rather than read it in her eyes.

I walked down the road thinking irritably about her and saying to myself, "Why can't she wait a couple of days? After that she'll be able to see him for the rest of her life." I stopped at the herbalist's to buy some dried yellow mushrooms. After that I looked for the map and the compass (of course, I didn't find them) and the old slave's strange behavior completely vanished from my mind.

When I arrived back at the inn I found it the scene of noisy revelries.

On an outspread mat in the middle of the room, a wrestler was panting and struggling with a huge tame bear, standing on its hind legs. The onlookers were encouraging them with wild shrieks and cries, and the din, combined with the tobacco smoke and the acrid smell of sweat and filth, was so intolerable that I whistled to Balyu and prepared to go outside again.

Suddenly a hand drew me aside. It was Abu Talib.

"Where are you going?" he asked, removing the long chibouk* from his mouth.

"It's very stuffy," I said.

"Come with me a minute," he said and led me towards the stables. I immediately realized that he had bought the horses.

"Thank you from the bottom of my heart, Abu Talib. Just in time . . . they're working on the wall now, you know."

"Did you see your father?"

"Yes, I saw him."

"Go inside," he said, opening the stable door. I stepped in, certain that I would see my three horses, but, to my great surprise, found myself confronted with camels. One of them slowly turned its head towards me, moved its lips and blinked.

"Are you pleased?" Abu Talib's eyes twinkled. "I got them cheap. There is some money left over."

"I'm pleased," I told him after I'd gotten over my astonishment.

To tell the truth, I had never been so displeased over anything in my life. What sort of animal was a camel for a getaway? With their fast, nimble-footed horses, the zaptiehs would overtake us in no time. Naturally, I could not tell Abu Talib this. I smiled with an effort, as I had now done so many times before.

"The trouble is, I don't know whether I'll be able to ride one, Abu Talib. It's six months since I rode with Selim Baba's caravan."

"Don't worry, Ali. After lunch, Allah willing, when the inn is empty, I'll show you how to handle a camel again. What's more, we'll go outside the city wall," he added significantly, and I realized that he was referring to the part of the wall which the prisoners were pulling down so as to rebuild it more securely a few days later.

As usual, Abu Talib was as good as his word.

When the afternoon sun dipped in the sky, he brought out two of the camels, and made them kneel down while we mounted them.

The road led south through the Mardin Gate. I had never been there before and I suddenly realized I had no pass. Only women were allowed out without one.

I mentioned this to the old man.

120 ◀

"Don't worry." That was what he always said, and it reassured me.

Indeed, everyone knew Abu Talib, and the city gates were opened for him. As I was with him, they were opened for me too, and half an hour later we were out on the Mardin road. Actually it was not a road at all, but a steep stony path which disappeared among the rocks and must have led to the very foot of the towering snow-capped mountain.

"Where did you decide to make for?" the Arab asked suddenly.

"I don't know. My brother . . ." I nearly fainted from fright, but luckily Abu Talib was busy with his camel and paid no attention to what I was saying. "That is, my father," I quickly amended, "told me to find a map for the journey. But there aren't any. As for compasses, no one has even heard of them."

"Compass, what's that?" he asked.

Now I had said something else I shouldn't have. What would a simple Turkish peasant boy know about compasses?

"You can tell the direction from it, Abu Talib."

"Oh," he said. "The direction! And what is the sun for, young man? And the stars at night? Wait, stop a minute."

I reined in my camel and came to a halt. He turned around and drew alongside me, feeling all the while for something in his belt.

I sat and waited. A soft spring breeze fanned my face and cheered me. How many months was it since I had been outside those walls? How freely one breathed out here although the surroundings, as far as the eye could see, were uniformly bleak and desolate. But no, not completely desolate. From this side of the wall, right down to the bottom of the hill, stretched the cemetery of the Armenian Christians. There was green shrubbery there and some trees, whose blossoming branches stood out in bright relief against the somber black rocks.

"Look, Ali!"

Abu Talib unfolded a thick sheet of crackling paper for me to see.

"I have sketched out the route for you. Now look, this dot here is our town. If you go due south, along the road we are on now, you will come first to Mardin village. It is over there, see, just below the mountain peak."

I looked where he was pointing, and looked back at the map he had drawn. Dear, kind Abu Talib—when had he done all this for me? I saw that the lines had been drawn with an unsteady hand and the place-names were written in somewhat uneven Arabic letters, for the old Arab was not very skilled in writing.

He turned his camel further around so that I should have a better view, and continued, "From Mardin onwards there is only one road. It goes east through Nisibin and Mosul, all the way to Baghdad. But don't you be misled into taking it, my boy. The zaptiehs could still catch you there! Carry on south as far as Chebrisa. Do you see where I have marked Chebrisa? That's it; that's where the desert begins. See, it's marked here. Go down this river. It's usually dry, but let's hope you are lucky, as it's springtime now. Stay on it and it will take you out into the Euphrates," he said, pointing with his fingernail to the thickest wavy line on the piece of paper. "The Euphrates is a big river, Ali, like our Tigris, only even bigger. When you get there, you'll have to cross it. You're sure to find a way; then keep on this road I've marked for you. There, in the middle of the desert, is an old deserted fort. Once you are there, the worst will be over. You will already be in Syria. Only from there on, you should not head for Sham,[1] but cut through the mountains. And see here where I have drawn this little circle? That is the port of Tripoli. When you get there, look for a merchant named Hedi Zegal, a fat man always laughing. I have written down his name so that you won't forget. He-di Ze-gal," he read out slowly, one syllable at a time. "You will say, Abu Talib from Diyarbakir sent me. You don't have to tell him anything else. He will find you a boat and, what is most important of all, you need not be afraid that he will give you away. He is a Moslem, a firm believer in the true faith. That's it, Ali! Can you remember it all?" he asked as he handed me the piece of paper.

---

[1] Sham: Damascus.

I seized his hand and kissed it. "I shall always remember you in my prayers, dear Abu Talib!"

"And I shall miss you, Ali. I've grown fond of you, son. As Allah is my witness, I shall find it hard without you."

I had the impression that his eyes misted over, but perhaps it was just the effect of the spring breeze.

He prodded his camel and rode off down the winding path between the sharp rocks until the crosses of the Armenian cemetery barred the way.

I carefully folded the sketch, tucked it in my belt and went after him.

"Remember the way, Ali!" he called, turning round in his saddle.

Why did he say that? Oh, of course! This was the way we would have to go the day after tomorrow, to get to the Mardin road.

I carefully surveyed the surroundings. How would I remember them? That rock on the left was so thin and sharp that it looked like a bird's beak. And there were two olive trees side by side over there. Trees were such a rarity in these parts that one could not help remembering them. Nonetheless my hopes were placed in Balyu who, as usual, was trotting at my heels.

We rounded two or three more turns; then the path suddenly branched out into several narrower ones, through which the camels could barely squeeze.

Abu Talib turned to me again.

"Now, look over there on the left. Do you see anything?"

"What is there to see? The path ends there. That is all I can see," I told him.

The innkeeper's grizzled beard quivered and tilted up. From his eyes I could tell that he was chuckling to himself and was pleased about something.

"As Allah is my witness, that is just what I wanted to hear you say, Ali. It comes to an end, eh? That's right; the path ends but a cave begins. Tomorrow, as soon as they open the city gates, I'll bring the three camels, with their packs, to that very cave. Now, do you understand? It should not be on the exact day of your escape, because someone might notice them.

I shall leave them here, and towards evening we'll go and take a look at them."

"But what if someone finds them?"

"No one will find them, Ali. Rest assured, I know what I am doing. Besides, can't you see what is going on in town? Bedlam! Who is going to come out here at a time like this?"

As usual, he showed foresight and wisdom. But I confess that I was afraid and full of forebodings. If the camels spent the night out here, would I find them the next morning? Furthermore, what would become of my brother and Bai Nestor?

As we rode down the slope, my mind kept returning to this thought. It was odd that I should be so obsessed by it. I had lived through so many dangers that I felt quite inured to them; yet this uncertainty frightened me more than any zaptieh. I said nothing to Abu Talib, but inwardly I carried on an entire conversation. Should I agree or shouldn't I? Should I come to the cave tomorrow and guard the camels until the following day? Or should I consult Meira? Perhaps the two of us would find some solution.

The last alternative seemed the most acceptable. Besides, I had begun to think about Meira, about the look I had seen in her eyes today, and the fact that I was supposed to visit them in the evening. How would the two of them get out

of the fortress, I wondered, then answered my own question—
they would get out all right. Women did not carry passes and
no one ever stopped them at the gate.

The rocks on both sides of us gradually thinned out until
they disappeared among the crosses of the graveyard, which
began at this point.

"Let's hurry!" Abu Talib said grimly, giving his camel a
sharp dig in the flanks.

Picking our way among the crosses and graves, we quickly
crossed the cemetery and found ourselves near that part of
the fortress where the prisoners had been working. As I had
imagined, a long stretch of wall had already been torn down.
Although I looked all around, I could see no sign of the
prisoners.

"They are not there," I said, betraying my apprehension.

Abu Talib followed the direction of my gaze and, seeing
what I meant, remarked with a smile, "Look at the sun and
you will see why they were taken back. We will have to
hurry ourselves, Ali, since it will soon be dark."

I nodded and followed him in silence. When we approached
the Urum Kapia,* the guards were already calling:

"Oh, faithful! Faithful! It is said that the day is for work
and the night is for rest! Blessed be Allah who has decreed
when man shall labor and when he shall rest!"

The gate creaked and then someone shouted, "Don't close it, that is Abu Talib!"

We spurred on our camels and a minute later we were inside the town. The iron gate clanged behind us and the chain rattled. There was a babble of voices. All these sounds brought back eerie memories of that fateful day when I first set foot in the fortress. I had called it a trap then. A grim and terrible trap it was even now, but something had changed—both the times and I had changed. I no longer felt afraid and I was not entirely without hope.

Chapter 11

A Sad Night

THAT EVENING ABU TALIB AND I BROUGHT OUT all the things I had stored in the little shed over the past few months. We sorted them into separate piles and prepared them for loading. I was terrified that some object might give me away.

"What do you need those revolvers, those guns for?" the innkeeper asked at one point.

"Oh, well, anything can happen, Abu Talib. Even in the desert there are bad people, aren't there?"

"That's true. There are bad people everywhere," he said and dropped the subject of the firearms, although a little later, I saw him shake his head uneasily.

"What is it, Abu Talib?" I asked nervously.

"You have accumulated a lot of things, son. What do you need them for? There are only two of you. Let's see now, you will need water, rusks, and fodder for your camels. But the two of you won't be able to manage with three animals. If the zaptiehs track you down, you will never escape their clutches."

➤ 127

"That is why I suggested horses."

"No, forget about horses! Quite apart from their endurance, surely you don't think that camels are slower than horses. Listen, Ali, you will have to take one more camel."

"Today was market day, Abu Talib. It's too late now. We can't . . ."

The old man would not let me finish. "I'll give you one of my camels," he said, not looking at me. "I'll give you my fastest one, which is faster than a Nejdee horse."*

I was deeply moved. "Abu Talib!"

"Don't, don't, son! There is no need to thank me. Let it be a keepsake from me. Now, let us go to bed, as it is late. Tomorrow we shall load the camels and, as soon as they open the gates—off to the cave! No, you are not coming with me. I shall take them myself. It's better that way; nobody will suspect old Abu Talib. Sleep well, Ali," he added, starting towards his little room at the back of the inn. Pretending I had to feed the dog, I went out into the yard.

A quarter of an hour later, Balyu and I were speeding along the dark winding streets towards Feisal Bey's house. We climbed the hill leading to the back garden. I gave the door a push. It was open, so I went in, leaving Balyu outside.

Once again, I saw no sign of the big dog, but I could just barely hear it barking out front. No doubt Meira had seen to that. No matter even if I had run into the dog, for it already knew me by now. Anyway it was not the dog, but Feisal Bey that I was afraid of. Luckily the windows of his house were in darkness. He was probably snoring away amongst his stout wives and, at that moment, I wished with all my heart that he might never wake again.

I carefully shut the door behind me and set off towards the huts. The slender crescent of the new moon lit the way. I sprinted from bush to bush, taking cover behind the cypresses as I approached.

I had never come at such a late hour. Lilliah might have gone to sleep, but her mother would be waiting, I knew.

I skirted Toparlak Bekir's hut. Like the handsome windows of the house, his too were in darkness. What could the funny old eunuch be dreaming about, I wondered. I had never been curious about his nationality, how he came to be here, who had sold him into slavery or why he had been maimed for life. Now, suddenly, for some reason, these questions came crowding into my mind. It grieved and pained me to think how joyless his life must be.

As I expected, there was a light in the window of Meira's hut. A faint, barely discernible light, but a light nonetheless. I hurried towards it, anticipating the joy I would see on the faces of the two women.

A tattered curtain at the window was fluttering in the soft breeze and, as I passed, I happened to glance in. In the half-dark I could just make out the shape of a back. It was not a woman's back!

I stopped and peered in. The curtain flapped again, shutting off my view, but revealing the other half of the interior. I saw the opposite wall and the candle, which was set on a high shelf as usual. On the matting on the floor, lay a figure, whose fitful groans mingled with the sound of quiet, weary weeping.

A woman's voice, not Meira's, not Lilliah's, said, "Don't cry, little one, it will not help. Fate must take its course."

"Allah is merciful!" I heard the shrill voice of Toparlak Bekir cry. Evidently it was his back I had glimpsed.

I listened, not understanding a word. But still I did not move. The feeling of buoyancy, of triumph with which I had come suddenly turned to anxiety. Who was groaning? Who was weeping? What was the meaning of the words spoken by the strange woman and by Toparlak Bekir?

Again I heard the sound of a woman's voice. Wasn't that Fatima Kadin, the oldest of the slaves?

"Dip the cloth in the vinegar, dear," she was saying. "Wet it and put it on her forehead. Doesn't that feel better, sister?"

The groaning continued.

"Let us go," said Toparlak Bekir and, as the curtain shifted again, I saw that he was standing up.

"You do as Fatima Kadin tells you, and, if the worst happens, you know where we are, call us right away. But keep quiet," he added, "you know that the master is beside himself."

I hastily moved away, hid behind the hut, and waited for them to come out. They soon appeared in the doorway, said something as they stood there that I could not catch, then started off down the path towards the other hut.

"She won't pull through," I heard Fatima Kadin say softly as she passed by me. "It will be a miracle if she lasts till morning."

The eunuch murmured something then. As a gust of wind blew in my direction, I caught the words: "She said we should take her to the infidel cemetery and not bother about her any more."

They disappeared behind an outbuilding. I heard a door open, then another.

Now, I could enter the hut myself.

As Lilliah and I knelt beside the dying Meira, Lilliah, through her tears, told me what had happened.

That morning when they had learnt from me that the prisoners were working on the wall and that Bai Nestor was one of them, no power on earth could keep the two women away. Moreover, the bey had gone out.

Toparlak Bekir was easily taken in. They told him that they were going to the market, to look rather than to buy anything, for how much money would a slave be likely to carry?

And off they went.

"Oh, if only we had never gone!" sobbed Lilliah, dissolving into tears.

Instead of making for the market, they had set off for the Urum Kapia, along the same streets I had traveled myself, early that morning.

The prisoners, in their chains and covered with black dust, had still been working on the wall.

Mother and daughter had spent a long time trying to pick out their man from among the scores of exiles. They gazed at them all in turn but did not see him.

Of a sudden, a voice thundered behind them, a voice that they knew only too well. It struck terror to their hearts.

"Who are you, women? Don't you belong to me?"

Perhaps Feisal Bey had recognized them from their yashmaks. Or perhaps he had expected to see them there. Who knows? Anyway, the next minute their fear betrayed them. They took to their heels and ran so fast, so desperately that, as soon as they entered the garden, they both collapsed on the grass and lay there completely exhausted.

Eventually, they got back to the hut somehow, reassuring each other that everything was all right. A quarter of an hour later, however, the bey came bursting in.

"I'll kill both of you!" he roared, brandishing a short stout club and raining blows on them. "So you haven't forgotten that vile infidel? Take this, and this . . ."

And he beat them and beat them until Meira, who was shielding her daughter, finally fell to the floor, covered with blood.

The bey stopped then and stepped back a pace, and eyed her suspiciously. She might be pretending, although she was bleeding from her nose and mouth, and her disordered gray hair was soaked in blood.

"Go on, pretend!" he cried, a note of alarm in his voice. Perhaps he recalled at that point how many gold liras he had once paid for her.

He flung down the blood-stained stick and made for the door. "Tomorrow I'll sell the two of you to Hadji Hassan, just you see!" he threatened from the doorway. "No, you're old, I'll sell you, and I'll take your daughter into my harem. Tomorrow, you hear! Go on, get up, that's enough shamming!"

But poor Meira lay there on the bare earthen floor, and neither his threats nor her daughter's tears had any effect on her.

Meira was no longer bleeding, but she continued to groan and to stare into space. While her daughter had been speaking, Meira twice turned her face towards us. Whether she saw us or recognized us I could not tell.

"Look after her, Nestor. Don't let him get her, Nestor."

"Mother, mother, it's I, Lilliah. Father isn't here. Just Rali and I."

Again she said, "Look after her, Nestor. Don't let him get her, Nestor." Then her voice trailed off and the pitiful moaning began again.

A moment later for the first time, I detected a gleam of recognition as her eyes rested on us.

"Lilliah, run away! Lilliah, run, my child!"

There was a pause. Then she said to me, "Rali! Is that you, Rali? Take her to her father, my boy. Get away, both of you . . . far away . . . far away. Tell . . . tell him that for his sake . . . for his sake, I . . . ."

A great shudder passed through her body. She doubled up, stiffened and then suddenly lay still.

"Mother!" Lilliah seized her in her arms.

I remained on my knees, motionless, the tears streaming down my face. My father had been killed, and my mother and sister had been burnt alive. But I had not been there to see. Now, for the first time, someone close to me had died before my eyes.

I remember that for a long time Lilliah and I stayed silently beside her mother's body. At last from the neighboring gardens came the crowing of a rooster. Then the light began to filter through the curtain. It was daybreak.

"Lilliah, didn't you hear what she said? You must run," I said.

"I heard."

"Today, Lilliah! If you don't run away today, Feisal Bey will lock you up in his harem."

"How can I leave her, Rali?" she asked sorrowfully.

I kept still. How could she leave her mother so soon?

"Listen, then," I said, turning to her. There was enough light from the window and the candle still burning in the hut for me to see her face, and I scarcely recognized it—it was so gray and drawn.

"This is what you must do, Lilliah. After, well, you know . . . your mother will have to be buried. The eunuch said that he would take her to the Christian cemetery."

"She was a Christian, like father," said Lilliah, although I knew this perfectly well. "I am a Christian, too," she added fiercely.

I looked towards the window. It was growing lighter every minute. What if Feisal Bey suddenly appeared, or Toparlak Bekir? I had to hurry, hurry!

We stood up.

"After the burial, hide among the graves," I told her. "The eunuch will think you have gone on ahead. Then go up to the rocks where the path to the Mardin road begins. Do you know the path I mean?"

"No, I don't."

I groaned.

"Don't worry, I'll find it," Lilliah said shortly. "What shall I do there?"

"We will pass by there."

I could see from her blank expression that she did not understand.

"We—your father, my brother and I."

"Oh, Rali!" she cried, as if just awakening from a dream. "We're running away!"

"Of course we are running away! The camels will be there."

"What about horses?"

"There aren't any," I said. "Abu Talib has bought camels. He even gave me one of his own."

I was about to tell her how things had changed and how kind Abu Talib was being to me, when the cockcrow sounded again from the neighboring yard. Snatching up my fez, I rushed to the door.

➤ 133

"Can you remember everything? Don't forget to be near the path leading to the Mardin road."

"I'll remember, Rali."

I was starting to leave when I remembered that I had not paid my respects to the dead. I turned back, bent over and kissed the folded hands, and it was just as if I were kissing my own mother's hands.

"Go and wake Toparlak Bekir," I said to Lilliah, who had burst into tears again.

"It's early yet."

"No, go on," I insisted.

If she woke him early, he would take the body to the cemetery all the sooner. I did not have the heart to tell Lilliah that.

Chapter 12

The Flight

WHEN I AWOKE NEXT MORNING, MY FIRST THOUGHT was that I had overslept. Today of all days! How could I have overslept today?

I have never got dressed more quickly in my whole life. I snatched up the can with the mushrooms that had been soaking overnight in the boza and raced down the stairs.

Yakub, the servant, was sprinkling the floor with a little watering can and sweeping it listlessly.

"Where is your master?" I asked anxiously.

He turned his head towards me and leaned against the wall. "The master has gone."

"Gone? Where?"

"I don't know myself. When I saw him he was leading four camels. 'I'll be back for lunch,' he shouted. That's all I know."

I took out a piece of paper and pencil and wrote:

"Thank you for everything, dear Abu Talib. It seems we have to leave right away. I shall always be grateful to you. Ali."

I did not fold the paper, while I stopped to think. I must write something more—it was really necessary. I added: "Please, Abu Talib, don't think badly of me."

"Give this to your master, Yakub. Mind you don't mislay it; it's very important."

I took out a silver coin, "And this is for you." I gave it to him with the letter.

He blinked, looked at me in surprise and started to bow.

"That's all right," I said and picked up the can. "One does not give in order to be thanked, but because one is grateful."

On the way I stopped to buy two meat pies. I ate one and gave one to Balyu. The man selling them opened his eyes wide and clicked his tongue. "Allah! Fancy giving a meat pie to a dog!" Then I bought some more and had them wrapped up in thick brown paper and went on my way.

I called at Feisal Bey's house, although it was not on my route.

The aged Fatima Kadin let me in.

"Is Toparlak Bekir there?" I inquired casually.

She blinked, came closer and lowered her voice. "No, he's not here, Ali. He went to take poor Meira . . ."

"Where has he taken her?" I asked, pretending not to understand.

"Oh, dear, I forgot that you did not know, son. A terrible thing happened. Poor Meira died. She is gone. She is out of her misery."

"But only yesterday she was alive and well, how can it be?"

She glanced back towards the garden. "Out of her misery," she repeated. "Whatever happens to a poor slave like us, that's what we say, 'out of her misery.'"

"And Lilliah?"

"Lilliah is mourning, son."

"But isn't she here?" I asked in alarm.

"How could she be here, Ali? What are you saying? She went with Toparlak Bekir to see her mother to her last resting place. The master would not let us out, son. He didn't want her to go either, but then he said, 'All right, let her go! When she comes back she shall go straight into my harem,'

He will blight her young life for good. No doubt of that."

"Where is Feisal Bey. Is he here?"

"He's over there in the selamlik, drunk. Don't imagine he is grieving for Meira. No, it's the ten liras he is fretting over. That is what he paid for her at the time. But who knows? Surely he has a soul, even if it is an evil one. 'That hound Nestor!' he cried. 'I'll kill him too! This very day I shall go and ask the Pasha to let me have him.' Oh, why am I telling you all these things? You don't know Nestor or any of them. What is it, have you brought some boza?"

"No, not today. I came for the money, but since Toparlak Bekir is not here, never mind. I'll stop by tomorrow."

And I went away.

Now I had another reason for hurrying—Feisal Bey. He was a threat both to Lilliah and to Bai Nestor. Abu Talib had been right in saying that he could kill a man without batting an eyelid.

From the bey's house to the city wall, the road ran downhill, and in about ten minutes I was there. The guards recognized me from the day before and did not stop me. With Balyu's help I easily found the two prisoners I was looking for.

"Did you put the mushrooms in the boza?" whispered Bai Nestor.

Poor man, he had no inkling of what had befallen him during the night. I dared not look him in the face.

"Yes, I did."

"Now, go and offer a drink to those fellows up in the tower."

"Is the boza poisoned now?"

He shook his head and I chanced to look into his eyes—large, feverish, still youthful eyes, like Meira's.

"We are human beings and all we want is our freedom," he said. "We are not murderers . . ."

My brother nodded. "It will only put them to sleep, Rali. Hurry up and come back. We'll be waiting for you right by the wall."

I climbed the steps to the tower, came out on the platform and leaned against the brass cannon.

"Anyone thirsty up here?" I shouted at the top of my voice. "Boza! Spicy boza!"

The zaptiehs, posted at the embrasures to watch for any prisoners trying to escape, started to look around. One of them was an old acquaintance of mine.

"How much is it?" asked a tall mangy-looking Anatolian, with mustaches drooping over his jaws, evidently the thirstiest.

"Only two aspers, aga."

I deliberately set a high price.

"That's a lot," objected my old acquaintance from the prison. "Last year we only paid you one asper."

"Ah, you should have told me it was you, Babadjan," I told him, grinning. "All right, just to please you I'll let it go for one asper."

I filled first one mug, then another. "Who wants to be first?"

Babadjan drank first, then the tall Anatolian. But the third guard, to my dismay, had no money.

"I'll let you have it on credit," I offered.

He shrugged his shoulders. "What credit, lad? I've used up my pay for the next three months. Never mind, I don't want to make life difficult for you too."

"Since you're so considerate, I won't be outdone, aga. Here, let it be my treat!" and I impatiently thrust the refilled mug into his hands.

"Well, look at that!" the others protested. "Mültek gets it free and we have to pay. You'd think we were in the service of the Russian Tsar!" they joked. "Come on, stand us a drink too."

At first, I pretended to be reluctant, then finally gave in. I poured Mültek a second helping too. "Allah commands us to be just," I said. After he'd drunk it, I raced back down the stone steps. On my way, I stopped to offer a mug to each of the zaptiehs who were patrolling the other side of the wall and, lastly, to the one nearest my two prisoners.

"Now wait a while," whispered Bai Nestor, as soon as I came up. Apparently he had not taken his eyes off me the whole time.

"You go first," whispered my brother. From his voice I could tell that he was even more excited than I was. "We have filed through the chain and, as soon as we are outside the wall, we'll drop it."

"I'll wait for you in the cemetery. Bai Nestor, do you know the cemetery?"

"Yes. Is my wife there?"

I gave a start, then said quickly, "I've made all the arrangements."

Fortunately he was looking up at the tower; otherwise my face would have betrayed me.

I heard him say, "Those fellows are dozing already. Ah, so is ours!"

And, sure enough, the nearest guard was resting with both hands on his gun. He began to nod, then jerked to attention, then dropped his head again.

"Here, Rali!" ordered my brother. I went up to him in some trepidation. Had the time come at last? He gave me a stern, searching look. His eyes said, "This is it. It's freedom or death."

I picked up the can and, whistling to Balyu to follow me, walked through the gap in the wall and found myself outside the fortress.

No one shouted at me. No one stopped me. Were there any guards outside, I wondered.

I quietly set down the can among the boulders and, keeping close to the wall to hide in its shadow, hurried up to the cemetery. Another hundred paces and I was lost among the crosses and bushes. I stopped for a moment and looked around. Balyu was coming. But where were they? There was no sign of them. Perhaps they were hidden in the shadow of the wall.

I was shaking all over. What on earth should I do now?

First of all, I'd better look for Lilliah.

"Go seek!" I ordered Balyu, holding under his nose a scarf of Lilliah's that I'd had the foresight to pocket the night before.

He sniffed it, looked at me and promptly darted off among the graves. I hurried after him, alternately calling his name

➤ 139

and the girl's. The tombstones got in the way. I jumped over them, dodging the crosses. Then I shouted again, "Balyu, here! Lilliah! Where are you, Lilliah?"

I do not know which of us saw her first, Balyu or I. She was lying over the soft earth of a freshly dug grave and, when she first looked at me, her eyes were so distant and so strange that I was afraid she might have lost her reason.

"Where is Toparlak Bekir? Why are you still here?" I scolded, breathlessly. "Why aren't you in your place by the path?"

She looked at me as if she didn't know what I was talking about.

Then, suddenly, she recognized me. "Rali! It's you, Rali!" And she flung herself into my arms, weeping.

"I hid until now, as you told me, but I couldn't stay. I had to come back. I'll never see her again, Rali, never. You don't know what it is . . ."

"I know, Lilliah. Has Toparlak Bekir gone?"

"He's gone. I hurried on ahead and he raced after me, trying to catch up."

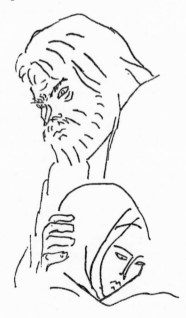

"You don't think he might come back to look for you, do you?"

She drew back quickly and, if I hadn't kept a firm hold on her, she would have run away.

"What is it? What's wrong?" I felt with my free hand for the revolver, hidden in my belt.

"Men! I heard footsteps!"

I could not see the men yet, but Balyu's bark of joy told me who was coming.

"Stop! Wait! That's my brother Lukan and your father, Lilliah!"

"My child, my little one..." was all I could hear, as two long firm arms seized her and held her tight.

The next moment I heard nothing at all for I, too, was gripped in a fierce bear hug. "Rali, my little brother!"

"Bate!"

For a whole year I had waited for that moment. For a whole year I had looked forward to that hug.

"Your mother? Where is your mother?" I heard Bai Nestor ask Lilliah anxiously.

I quickly broke away from my brother's grasp and looked at Lilliah.

"Mother, she . . ." Her eyes filled with tears and she could not continue.

"Why are you crying, child? What is it? Don't torture me; someone tell me! Rali?"

"There is your Meira," I murmured, as his daughter dropped to her knees beside the grave.

At first I thought that Bai Nestor had not heard me. There was a look of bewilderment and of disbelief in his eyes. How was it possible—Meira? But all of a sudden his care-worn face became contorted with pain; he shuddered and gave a terrible groan. Then he flung himself on the grave and began sobbing so violently, so bitterly that, although it is hard to admit it now, I shrank from the sight. I found it embarrassing and, in my childish way, repugnant. Could a man really sob like that, a man who had held a gun in his hand and had rotted in prison for twenty years without succumbing?

How inexperienced I was then! And how true it is that each age understands only its own feelings!

"Oh, oh!" he moaned. "I never saw you, my love, my faithful one . . . Day and night I kept thinking of you, kept thinking all the time. You were all I had left. And now you have gone, my dearest."

Something in him had given way. He was a broken man.

I remember that, like me, my brother did not stir, and I wondered if he felt as I did.

"Get up, Bai Nestor, get up!" Lukan said, in a few moments, taking him gently by the shoulders.

"Leave me alone! Leave me . . ."

"We are not leaving you, brother. I know, I understand, but we must run. You have a daughter, don't forget!" Lukan added with sudden severity, although his eyes were full of tears. "Any minute now, they might discover we are missing."

"Let's run, father," Lilliah urged and jumped up.

Since last night she had pulled herself together. Now, she was thinking of her father as well as of herself.

"Quick! Feisal Bey may come here!" she cried in horror.

"Feisal Bey?" Bai Nestor lifted his head. The sound of that

name brought him back to life. "What? Feisal Bey?"

"He killed her, father! Yesterday. He killed her. He wanted to kill me too!"

He jumped up and clasped her fiercely to him. "Let him come. I'll kill *him!*"

I thought he had gone mad.

"Come with me, Bai Nestor," said my brother and took him firmly by the arm.

"Where is he? Where is that murderer? Let me get at him," repeated the old man, pulling away.

"Come!" My brother pushed him roughly. "Lilliah, take his other arm. Rali, lead the way."

He rapped out orders briskly. Strangely enough, although it was hardly the time for reminiscences, I was reminded of the old days. He had been just as resolute and commanding at school, at the secret meetings of the committee, and when leading his group of rebels during the uprising.

I gave him my revolver. It would be better in his hands.

I set off, with the other following me.

I soon found the path, but where was the cave? "A tall boulder, sharp as a beak," I repeated to myself. But there were many boulders along our route, all tall and all sharp. Then I remembered the olive trees. There were two of them, side by side. Two, yes, but where were they? I was ready to weep with frustration when my brother seized me by the shoulder and stopped me.

"Look, over there! What's that?"

I turned round. He was pointing at some shrub, whose name I didn't even know.

"Look at what?"

"Those yellow hairs on that shrub are off a camel."

"Off a camel?"

It all came back to me in a rush. "Go back!" I shouted. "We have to turn off to the right. There, down that track!"

We turned right and, soon afterwards, the two gnarled olive trees came into view. A little further on we found the cave.

The camels were there.

Thank God, there was no Abu Talib.

At once, Lukan and Bai Nestor, who had grown calm but was so dazed and unsteady that we had to keep helping him, slipped on their Kurdish headdresses, strapped on the guns, and we led the camels out of the cave. Seconds later we were riding up the path and then along the Mardin road. The poor animals snorted at every step, bellowing in protest, but we goaded and whipped them relentlessly, shouting to each other, "Hurry! Faster!"

Not until we reached the top of the steep hill where the road began to wind into the mountain, did Lukan halt his frothing camel and turn it around. We did the same.

Down below, at our feet, the Tigris River slithered through the valley of black stone like an overstuffed snake. Opposite us lay the jagged outline of the wild Taurus mountains and on one side, on the slope, Diyarbakir. From where we stood, the city wall looked tiny and forlorn. We could also see the inner wall, belonging to the prison. But where was Abu Talib's inn? And Feisal Bey's mansion?

I looked hard but could not locate them.

Just then a thunderous report reached our ears. It was like the sound of rocks hurled from a great height. Again and again, the echo resounded. We listened expectantly. There it was again.

"The cannon," said Bai Nestor, and his pale face seemed to turn paler if that was possible.

"Why are they firing it?"

"It's the signal that prisoners have escaped," he said in a barely audible voice, glancing at his daughter.

"We have a good start," declared my brother quickly, but I had the impression that he said this not so much because he believed it as to reassure Lilliah and me. "It will take them all day to decide what to do and where to go."

Nevertheless, we hurriedly spurred the camels and soon the awesome black fortress was hidden from view.

I brought out the package of meat pies and handed them round.

"Take one," I said, "and let's hope this is our last taste of Diyarbakir."

Part III
In the Desert

Chapter 13

El Shakhin

I HAD OFTEN HEARD ABU TALIB SAY, "NO MAN CAN escape the fate that Allah has decreed."

But here were the four of us—two men sentenced to banishment for life, one young slave and I, not yet fifteen—who had no intention of living the life that had been decreed for us. Freedom—that was our goal! That was what gave us strength, determination and hope.

All through the night we rode south. At dawn we passed the snowy Mardin peak and the road, instead of growing easier, became twice as hard. The descent was steep and was scored with gullies, and the camels often stumbled, stopped and refused to move.

We men dismounted and continued on foot. Only Lilliah stayed on her camel. She, poor girl, being unused to riding, was worn out from the journey as well as last night's ordeal, and kept dozing and starting awake, tormented by nightmares.

Her father led her camel as well as his own. Occasionally in the half-light I would catch the sad expression on his face and think: the last time he saw his daughter she was ten years old and now she is nearly sixteen.

The early morning breeze ruffled her feredje* and blew out her veil and I discovered to my surprise that she was no longer a child but had grown into a shapely young woman, who could even be called beautiful. I do not know why, but I was pleased by this beauty of hers, and proud. I said to myself, "It is my doing that she is not going into the harem of that beast Feisal Bey today."

When the sun rose we saw a rocky desert spread before us, not black like the land around Diyarbakir, but grayish-yellow, the color of ashes. Scattered about were patches of wiry steppe grass and stunted bushes.

The road between them could hardly be seen, but Lukan, who, of course, was leading us, did not look that way. He kept turning around and looking back at the steep slopes we had come from.

"Any sign of them, teacher?" Bai Nestor would inquire from time to time.

"Not a sign."

"Thank God!"

This convinced me that Abu Talib—I had talked to them about him at length and with great feeling—had been right. The zaptiehs would look for us on the shortest route to the sea—the road to Samsun—not the longest.

I told them this, several times.

"I don't know. I should think that, first of all, they would search the environs," my brother said finally.

Bai Nestor shook his head dubiously. After a while I heard him ask again, "No sign of them?"

"No sign."

"Thank God!"

Another hour went by. We were so overcome with fatigue that we could barely drag our feet, and the sun was getting hotter and hotter.

"Can't we ride now?" I pleaded.

"It would be better if we all had a rest," said my brother.

We found a shady spot by some round rocks with a view of the road to Mardin. We were famished. After eating a quick meal and drinking half the water in one of the skins, we stretched out on the warm ground. Lukan and Bai Nestor filed away at the iron rings which they still wore round their ankles, Lilliah fed Balyu, and I was supposed to be watching the mountain for any sign of our pursuers but, somehow or other, I dozed off.

I was awakened by a swift tap from Lilliah's cool fingers.

"What is it?" I said with a start.

"Get up! They are coming!"

I leapt up and immediately reached for the small revolver which Lukan had returned to me, keeping the two big ones for himself.

Lilliah pointed to my brother and Bai Nestor. They had clambered up among the boulders and were surveying the stony plain. The plain, mind you, not the steep slopes leading to the peak which we had come from, and the road to Diyarbakir.

This was puzzling.

"They haven't surrounded us, have they?" I whispered when I had reached the rocks beside them.

"No," my brother said, shaking his head. "I don't think

it's the searching party. There, do you see? Look between that slanting boulder and the sandhills. Three of them!"

I looked where he was pointing and I could see three men dressed in white—two on horseback armed with long rifles, and a third on foot. They were advancing slowly in our direction. Although they were still a long way off, I now saw that one of the horsemen was swinging his arm over the man on foot. The horseman was holding something in his hand. Why was he swinging it?

"He's beating him!" I whispered in astonishment.

"Yes. And the one being beaten—listen—he's singing!"

The desert wind surged over us in great warm waves, carrying with it the strains of a song, a high-pitched monotonous song without words, consisting solely of a prolonged and displeasing "AaaaH!"

Bai Nestor said, "I can't see the face of that man on foot very well, but judging from his veil I should say he was a Syrian. It looks as if they are taking him to the place we escaped from. The Syrians are rebelling too, lads, and they are paying dearly for it."

At those words, which put me in mind of our uprising the year before, my hand tightened on the revolver.

"Not you!" my brother stopped me. "We know our job. Bai Nestor, I am leaving the one in front to you. I'll take the one behind. Ah, now we can see them clearly! That hired thug has a whip in his hand. There he goes again, whipping. Does that remind you of your trek to Diyarbakir, old jailbird? I'll never forget mine," he added softly and with a venom that I had never seen in him before.

Bai Nestor was already taking aim at one of the horsemen with his gun.

"Fire!" snapped Lukan.

The reports from his revolver and Bai Nestor's rifle rang out simultaneously. When the smoke cleared away, we saw the man with the whip slide from his saddle. The singer made a wild dash for the rocks.

"I missed," groaned Bai Nestor. "I've forgotten how to shoot, Lukan."

My brother and I quickly emptied our guns at the horseman,

but I do not know whether we wounded him or not. He ducked behind the slanting boulder, skirted the sand hills and pelted up the road to Diyarbakir. There was no point in giving chase. And, anyway, none of us gave him another thought.

We started running towards the Syrian. I do not know whether he was afraid, but it seemed that, throughout the whole episode, he had not moved from his place in the rocks. He stood with his chain in his hands, waiting for us. Anyone who was an enemy of his enemy must be his friend!

He was a young man, about my brother's age, short but sturdy, with a thick growth of hair on his chest, a bony aquiline nose and a swarthy bearded face. His face, shoulders, chest and back were covered with weals and bruises. They had evidently beaten him all the way.

"Stranger," my brother said in Turkish when we were within speaking distance, "you are not of our faith or our nationality, but you have been abused like us and suffering makes men brothers. There is your oppressor"—he pointed to the slain zaptieh—"now you are free."

Lukan handed him the file he and Nestor had used to saw through the iron bands round their ankles.

The Syrian took the file but held on to Lukan's hand and tried to kiss it.

My brother pulled back in embarrassment. "What's your name and why are you here?" he asked.

"My name is El Shakhin," the Syrian answered. "If you want to know why they were banishing me I'll tell you frankly —for rebel activities against the Sultan."

"Let me embrace you, brother!" exclaimed Bai Nestor, seizing hold of him.

Then I, too, embraced El Shakhin, while Lilliah, who had come up, made a bow.

Since we shared the same fate, our roads were the same.

As soon as El Shakhin cast off the chain, we mounted the camels and rode off into the desert. The Syrian rode the dead zaptieh's horse. He also took the man's gun and cartridges, but refused to take the zaptieh's cloak although his own clothes were all tattered and stained with blood.

"You'll need it," I said in surprise. "You'll freeze during the night."

"To take an enemy's weapon is a proud act, but to take his clothes is shameful," he replied.

From the tone of his voice I could tell that it was better not to pursue the subject, so I said no more.

Behind us my brother was giving Lilliah a lesson in Bulgarian.

"Say, Bulgaria."

"Bulgaristan?"

"No, that's Turkish. Say, Bul-ga-ri-a."

"Bul-ga-ri-a," she repeated.

I repeated it with her under my breath. When would we finally get there?

Lukan continued with the persistence I knew so well from my schooldays. "Say, *Az sum bulgarka.*"

"What does that mean?"

He translated and she smiled for the first time since her mother's death.

"What kind of Bulgarian am I if I don't know Bulgarian?"

"You'll learn. You just have to apply yourself."

"He'll teach you, daughter," put in Bai Nestor. "He is a schoolmaster, a teacher. He has taught so many people, he should be able to teach you."

"He even taught me," I said, grinning at him from my saddle.

"True! I even taught Rali. Only the trouble with you, my boy, is that you weren't much good at school," he said, with a sharp look in my direction. Then his whole face lit up at the recollection.

I bent my head. My eyes smarted. Why did he have to say that now? Did he have to say it in front of everyone?

"It's happened at last!" cried my brother. "Do you see, Bai Nestor? He got us both out of prison, rescued Lilliah and now, just look, in a minute he'll be bawling."

I swallowed my embarrassment and tried to smile. Lilliah, who had been listening carefully, was flushed with excitement.

"How amazing!" she exclaimed. "I don't understand a word; yet it feels so natural, as if the language were a part of me. It's hard to describe. What is my name in Bulgarian— Lilliah?" she asked, turning her large dark eyes to my brother.

"Whatever it is in Circassian, it will be the same in Bulgarian," I said, eager to show off my knowledge.

"No, Rali, you are wrong," her father corrected me. "She was christened Lila in Bulgarian, after my mother. But Meira, God rest her, could not pronounce it in the Bulgarian way and always made it sound Circassian, Lilliah, Lilliah. I was never able to teach her."

"Well, in that case, let's call her Lila," I suggested.

"No! Let it stay the way her mother pronounced it. Let that remain of her mother, if nothing else," Bai Nestor said, his eyes misting over again. After that he did not speak for a long time.

We younger ones also stayed silent for a while. Then Lukan drifted into conversation with Lilliah again. She asked him a question; he replied. And so the time flew by.

From time to time, we would still look round to see if a search party was coming after us, but far less frequently than before. We decided that even if the zaptieh who had got away gave them a clue to us, it would not matter by the time he reached Diyarbakir. And by the time our pursuers reached this place, we would be well away to the south. Besides, in the desert, traces disappear quickly.

That day we passed at some distance two small villages with buildings of adobe, and we had the impression that nobody saw us. El Shakhin had come that way and knew the place.

"The people here are no good," he told us when the minaret of the second village was lost to sight. "They won't even give you a drop of water. I can't tell you what it would be like if they found out you are not Moslems. It is different at the fortress of Chebrisa. There is water there and we can even get food for the animals."

Indeed, the need for water and fodder had been growing more pressing by the hour. I had not provided nearly enough. Two of the four waterskins were empty before we had even finished watering El Shakhin's horse. The camels would last out a day or two longer, possibly more. But after we had portioned out the fodder in the evening, there would not be a grain left over for the next day.

So our hopes were pinned on the town of Chebrisa. On Abu Talib's map the little desert fort was marked by a tiny circle. I imagined that the circle contained an enormous spring surrounded by countless sacks of fodder for our camels.

"Let's hurry!" we kept saying, driven now not by the thought of the search party but by the knowledge that Chebrisa was somewhere ahead of us and we might sight it at any minute.

Eventually the sun, which had been with us all afternoon, dipped behind the sand dunes to our right. The desert glowed. Flame-gold haloes shimmered over the rocks. The shadows turned the color of rust and gradually the valley before us was enveloped in warm darkness.

The valley, but not the opposite hills. There the last rays of the setting sun picked out the low wall of the fortress, with two watchtowers stationed like sentries at the sides of the entrance. Beyond the wall, appeared the sharp outlines of minarets and the dome of a mosque.

"There it is, there's the fort!" Lilliah and I cried. "We've reached Chebrisa!"

Only El Shakhin showed no enthusiasm.

"What's the matter?" asked my brother.

"As soon as the sun goes down they will close the gates."

"Then let's hurry!"

But we had barely reached the foot of the hill when, from above, came the cry:

"Faithful! Faithful! It is said that the day is for work and the night is for rest! Blessed be the name of Allah, who has decreed when man shall labor and when he shall rest."

"Don't close the gate! We have come a long way!" El Shakhin called in despair at the top of his voice.

The only response was the clank of the chain. The gate slammed to and the same voice called from within, "It is said that he who comes after sundown is no guest for our house!"

There was no sense in knocking or pleading. That was how things were in those southern parts. They would reply, "It is said," or "What is the hurry? The world was not made in a day."

Consequently we couldn't enter the fort of Chebrisa. We couldn't continue our journey either, for where would we go without water or food for the animals! The desert lay ahead!

We decided to spend the night in the palm grove which we discovered over on the right, between the rising on which the fortress stood and the sand dune. There were only about fifty trees, standing some distance apart, but the ground between them was damp and overgrown with fresh grass and flowering shrubs, which was most welcome to our famished beasts.

"If there is grass there must be water too," said El Shakhin. "I'm going to have a look."

He took one of the empty skins and quickly vanished among the palm trees.

"Come, let's have a bite to eat and then the three of you lie down," said my brother. "I'll keep watch until midnight. Then I'll wake the Syrian."

"No, Lukan, wake me," objected Bai Nestor. "El Shakhin is more exhausted than any of us. Lilliah, come child, have something to eat."

But Lilliah was already asleep on the grass.

As he was covering her with his cloak, he said, "Never mind, let her sleep. Sleep will give her more strength than food will."

I ate quickly and was preparing to lie down when I suddenly thought of my dog.

"Bate, may I give Balyu a little bread? He's hungry, too."

Lukan did not look round but I thought that I detected a smile on his face. "All right, give him some."

"Balyu, Balyu!" I called softly.

No answer.

I whistled.

"He's off hunting hamsters. He can take care of himself, Rali. Don't worry about him!"

I was not worried at all. I simply missed my dog and very

much wanted to give him a piece of bread. So I went off to find him.

The flowering shrubs along the pathway smelled sweet. Exotic birds, hidden high among the long leaves of the palm trees, filled the still night air with their strange cries. The whole scene was so strange, had such an eerie fascination, that I felt as if I were walking in a dream. Now and then I glimpsed the pale face of the waxing moon through the trees. I imagined that she, too, was prowling through the forest and furtively eyeing me as I was eyeing her. And this increased my sense of unreality.

I was startled by a sudden noise in the shrubbery nearby. What could it be? Then I heard a whimper and a bark.

"Balyu, is that you?"

It was, but he came out only for a minute, then slunk back again into the shrubbery.

I ran after him. "Come here, I've brought you some food!"

He would not come back. I saw his white form streak through the grass and reappear at the far end of the oasis where the rocky hill led up to the fortress.

"What is it, Balyu? Have you found something?"

He paid no attention. When I stopped for a moment, I heard the sound of running water and realized that Balyu had found a spring.

I rushed over, flung myself on the ground beside Balyu and plunged my face into the cold stream.

As I lay there drinking, I said to myself, "Balyu found it, and he deserves a whole loaf of bread." I got up, my face dripping with water, and decided to go and find El Shakhin right away so that, while the others slept, the two of us could fill all the skins with fresh water.

I whistled to Balyu and was about to start back when I heard sounds coming from the road that led to the gates of Chebrisa. I skirted the rocks, came out into the open and listened. Horses' hoofs. The search party? It couldn't be! The zaptieh could not have reached Diyarbakir so soon.

The clatter grew louder. Not one or two, but dozens of horses were approaching. Perhaps the zaptieh had met horsemen on the way. They could have been searching for us near Mardin and he had run into them.

Common sense told me to run, so that I could alert the others as quickly as possible. Instead, for some reason, I warned Balyu not to bark and moved closer to the city gates.

Horsemen were appearing over the top of the rise, as if springing out of the ground, and galloping along the road toward Chebrisa. The moon was behind them and I could see only their dark outlines, but they looked so sinister and frightening that they sent shivers down my spine.

"Hey, open up!" one of them shouted.

Some rode up to the gates and started hammering on them. There was the sound of iron clanging against iron. A man appeared at the battlements above. A light flashed, then vanished again.

A sleepy voice replied, "It is said that he who comes after sundown . . ."

"Ox, don't give me that nonsense!" a horseman interrupted him. "Open the gate at once. I am Feisal Bey from Diyarbakir!"

I could not believe my ears—Feisal Bey!

"Whoever you are, I am not opening the gate," said the man overhead. "Those are my orders."

"Call your superior immediately! Wait! Did any giaours enter your town today?"

"I don't know."

"What do you mean, you don't know! Idiot! Two filthy prisoners, a young slave—*my* slave—and a boy of fourteen or fifteen disguised as a Moslem. All riding camels!"

"Camels, you say? Some people did come after sundown, but we wouldn't let them in."

"Where are they?"

"They must be somewhere around or somewhere not far off."

I could not stand it any longer. I started running towards the oasis, but I was in such a hurry that, before I had gone ten paces, I tripped on some roots and fell sprawling on the ground.

"Hey, who goes there?"

"Is anyone there?"

"Stop! Stop!"

Voices shouted behind me, shots rang out. But by then I was safely hidden by the rocks and the next minute I was inside the palm grove.

There I was met by my brother. "Rali! Quick! Where have you been?"

"The search party!"

"We realized it was. Quick, onto your camel!"

My camel was already kneeling and I leapt onto its back. It rose to its feet, swayed uncertainly, then stepped out smartly on its long legs.

"Feisal Bey!" was all I could say, gasping for breath. "Over there. . . . Feisal Bey!"

"What? Feisal Bey?" exclaimed Bai Nestor with a start, turning right around in his saddle.

"He's the leader of the party. They are looking for us!"

"Where is the brute? Lukan, you go on, I have a score to settle."

"You have a daughter," my brother interrupted sharply. "We are all staying together."

Bai Nestor groaned and bent his head.

"Follow me!" my brother commanded us as, whipping his camel, he headed south towards the dark sand dunes.

Lilliah, Bai Nestor and I galloped after him, El Shakhin bringing up the rear on the horse. He had never heard of Feisal Bey, but he knew other beys and he kept a tight grip on his gun.

Chapter 14

A Matter of Life and Death

I DO NOT KNOW TO THIS DAY WHETHER IT WAS because of the darkness or because we got away in time that our pursuers lost track of us that night. It is even possible that their horses were more exhausted than our camels.

Anyway, we shook them off. The next morning, when the great southern sun began to blaze overhead, we anxiously scanned the horizon. There was no sight of them.

"Thank God!" said Bai Nestor at last, crossing himself.

Lukan, Lilliah and I also crossed ourselves, but El Shakhin dismounted, turned to face south, knelt down and raised his arms in prayer.

"Let's keep away so that we don't disturb him," suggested my brother. "He has as much reason as we have to thank heaven."

We moved back where we could talk while we waited.

Lukan and Bai Nestor discussed what we should do. Lilliah gazed into the distance, and I listened to the voices beside me, while I watched the Syrian touch the sand with his forehead and raise his arms heavenwards, thinking to myself, "If only Abu Talib could see us now!" I so much wanted that wise man to realize that there was no need for Moslems and Christians to be enemies, that Bulgarians and Arabs, Circassians and Turks were all people, all brothers, just so long as they were real human beings.

But Abu Talib was far away and when we resumed our journey, I thought about him for a long time. I thought of the advice and the help he had given me and remembered that, without him, nothing would have come of our flight. Only one thing puzzled me.

How did Feisal Bey know so much about us?

Of course he could easily have guessed that his slave would run away with her father, and that they would be joined by the prisoner who was chained to Bai Nestor. But how did he know that we were on camels? And, above all, how had he found out about me—how old I was and that I was in disguise?

Someone had seen us. I was sure of it. Diyarbakir was teeming with people just now. I imagined that while we were at Meira's grave that someone, lurking behind the bushes, had had a good look at us. Why not Toparlak Bekir? He knew both Nestor and me. Yes, it was the eunuch! He had come back to look for Lilliah and had seen us then.

So everything was clear.

Everything? What about the camels?

I soon found an explanation for that too. Our road had led us quite near the Mardin Gate. Someone there had sighted travelers and later connected the travelers with the report carried by Toparlak Bekir, and perhaps with the news of El Shakhin's liberation as well. Yes, of course, that would also explain how they knew that we were traveling south. And anyone traveling south would have to go through Chebrisa.

I persuaded myself that this was true, because I wanted to believe it. Somewhere deep down inside me there was a nagging doubt. I had really never once thought that Abu Talib could have betrayed us after all, when he realized that the fugitives were giaours. He must certainly have found out, and he must have connected my special interest in Feisal Bey's house with the escape of his slave. But now when the thought struck me, I considered it wicked and unjust after all that Abu Talib had done for me. And I rejected it, thrusting it out of my mind. But I could not relax. Again and again, I went over the sequence of events, recalling all the details of our escape, looking for evidence and for fresh explanations.

Hours went by like that.

"Why are you so quiet, Rali? You're not ill, are you?" my brother asked anxiously at one point.

"I'm all right. I was just thinking about our escape."

"Stop it; don't think about the past any more!"

And, indeed, he himself was the best illustration of the maxim that there is a time and place for everything.

I have always admired my brother Lukan—not just because he is my brother, but because he is one of those people to whom I could trust my life with absolute confidence. He did not simply lead us across the desert; he also quietly but firmly encouraged us and raised our spirits by keeping the conversation going so that the journey would be easier.

He was especially kind to Lilliah.

At first I thought that he was giving her the most attention because she was the most inexperienced of us all. Later on I gradually began to feel that Lukan was not doing it just out of duty, but because he wanted to. Whenever Lilliah glanced at him or asked him a question, I noticed his face light up. Had he grown fond of her? Certainly anyone could grow fond of Lilliah. But I thought it comical, and I turned my head so that he would not see me smile, that a stern, practical man like my brother could be disconcerted by a look from that little Lilliah.

My brother led the way across the desert, heading due south, frequently consulting Abu Talib's map and encouraging us by his self-assured bearing. But we all knew that during the night we had lost our way and had not the slightest idea where we were going.

Meanwhile the day was wearing on. By lunch time it was so hot that I stripped to the waist.

"You'll get burnt!" El Shakhin warned, looking at my white freckled back. "You had better wear your veil."

I paid no attention. How could I be cooler with my head swathed like his? I'd suffocate! Soon my back was as red as a boiled lobster. First it began to smart and then it really hurt. Ashamed, I hastened to carry out the Syrian's advice and took refuge under my veil, leaving a single hole for my eyes. I peered through it to see if anyone was laughing at me.

To my surprise, I saw that El Shakhin had stopped his horse. He moistened the forefinger of his left hand and held it up above his head.

"What are you doing?"

"I'm trying to see if there's any sign of a wind," he replied, continuing to test. "If it blows up, the sand will cover our tracks."

"But what if it doesn't?"

"If it doesn't, things will be bad—very bad!"

I wet my finger, too, and held it up. No, no sign of a wind. Not even a breath. Just hot shimmering air, like the inside of a giant furnace.

"Bad," remarked Bai Nestor.

My brother scolded us all. "It *will* be bad if we stay in one spot. Get moving, quickly!"

We set off again. Before an hour had gone by, it was clear that we could go no further. The animals were staggering with fatigue. We, too, were wilting in our saddles. Even my brother, the strongest of us all, dozed off a couple of times.

"Listen, Lukan, let's take a rest," groaned Bai Nestor. "It's useless to try to go on in this heat. We are just making it hard on the animals."

"The horse won't go any further," said El Shakhin. "So far he has carried me, but I won't be able to carry him."

"Very well," my brother finally agreed. "We'll take a rest. Only let's find a suitable place. And I hope we can make up for lost time later on, when it gets cool."

We soon found a low rocky hillock, like a miniature fortress, which proved suitable. We lay down among the rocks and, as soon as we had each drunk a mug of water, promptly fell asleep.

Bai Nestor stayed up to keep watch, assuring us that older people needed less sleep. Besides, he promised that in an hour's time he would awaken Lukan. But fatigue such as ours makes no distinction between young and old. As we found out later, he soon began to nod, then fell fast asleep, so that our little fortress was left completely unguarded.

No, there was still one guard—Balyu!

His ferocious barking waked me. The first thing I noticed was that it was dark. Large bright stars hung in the sky. The moon was half hidden by little fleecy clouds.

"Get up! The zaptiehs!" I heard my brother shout. "We're surrounded. Quick!"

He rapped out a series of brisk orders, in Turkish and Bulgarian:

"El Shakhin, you take the eastern side."

"Bai Nestor! Stand guard on this side."

"Rali! Where are you, Rali?"

"Here I am," I said, going up to him.

"You fend them off at the south end. Look, here! You and I are back to back! Go on, quick, my boy!"

"What about me?" That was Lilliah. Her beautiful voice sounded flat, but she was no coward. I thoroughly admired her.

"You . . . you mind the animals, Lilliah. See that they don't run away at the sound of the gunfire."

I fetched the cartridges from my saddle bags and took up the position my brother had assigned to me.

The desert before me was bare, with almost no rocks, and slightly rippled by the wind. There were no dunes and no depressions. Then where were Feisal Bey's men?

I whistled to Balyu.

"A fine thing if you've misled us!" I scolded him.

On the side where my brother was posted, a voice bellowed in the distance, "Nestor, you infidel swine! Give yourself up at once, do you hear? If you don't surrender we will kill you as well as your daughter and all the others! Do you know who I am?"

In the darkness I saw Bai Nestor's thin shoulders quiver ominously.

"Come on, murderer!" he cried. "You have already taken one-half of my life, so come and take the other! Don't send your zaptiehs, coward, come yourself!"

Shots rang out. Bullets whistled over the rocks. Unable to bear the suspense, I bent double and started running towards the other side to see where the riders were.

"Stay at your post!" yelled my brother. "And keep down, do you hear?"

I crouched down obediently, but I still managed to see the search party. The zaptiehs had split up into two groups and were galloping at full speed in a wide circle round our stronghold, shooting recklessly in our general direction.

Lukan and El Shakhin were taking careful aim. As a result, two or three of the horses were now careening about without riders.

I returned to my post and waited, revolver in hand. The desert resounded with shots; bullets spattered against the rocks and whined shrilly overhead.

"Take cover! Take cover!" my brother kept warning us, keeping up a rapid fire with his two pistols.

"They are coming at you, Rali! Shoot!"

With wild shrieks, some fifteen horsemen came thundering towards the rocks where I had taken shelter. I fired, fired again, and again. A man fell, a horse whinnied and reared. I fired another shot. But what had happened to my leg? Why had it suddenly gone numb? Then something hit me, passing through my right shoulder and travelling downward. The next minute I felt my arm grow numb too. I dropped the revolver as an intolerable stab of pain sent me reeling backwards.

"Rali!" Lilliah's voice rang out.

"Rali!" echoed my brother's.

I wanted to answer them. My lips moved but no sound came out. How silly to die just for a shoulder, I thought. They might at least have hit me in the heart! And that was the last thought I had. Except that very far away, high above me, as if among the stars in the southern sky, I thought I heard someone weeping.

* * * *

When I came to, everything around me was still. Hadn't I died after all? No, that was a silly thought. I could feel my head and my back. I was lying on something hard. Overhead were the same stars and there was the moon with a mauve-brown cloud on one side. How beautiful everything was! How good to be alive! Or had it all been a dream?

I listened. There was no gunfire. Instead, someone was speaking in Turkish. Had they captured us? I tried to raise myself but felt as if a millstone were on my chest.

I lay back and tried to make out what they were saying. Perhaps I would find out what had happened to the others. Groundless fears! The language was certainly Turkish but the voice was my brother's.

"I imagined so; that's why I sent you," he was saying. From his tone of voice, I gathered that he was talking to El Shakhin. "That means that there are no posts to the north."

"No, there are none."

I was right; it was the Syrian.

"Then load the animals, fellows. I'll take Rali on my camel. Bai Nestor and Lilliah had better ride with you, El Shakhin, or we might lose each other in the dark. Let's head back towards Diyarbakir. Feisal Bey can patrol the south if he likes. Once we are out of here, we can decide how to continue our journey. Do you all agree?"

The three said they did and the next moment Lukan was bending over me.

"You take him by the legs," he said. "Take care, easy now."

"Bate!" I whispered, stretching out my uninjured hand.

He promptly dropped to his knees beside me.

"Rali! How do you feel? If you only knew what a fright you gave us."

Then the others gathered round me—Bai Nestor, Lilliah and El Shakhin.

"Where's Balyu?" I asked anxiously.

"Balyu is on guard! Shall I call him?"

"No, don't. Not till you're ready."

"Oh, so you heard?"

"I heard." I smiled. "Get on with the loading, quick! And load me too. I'm a bundle now. If you put me in the saddle, there I'll be. If you don't, I'll stay here."

"Now, now!" admonished my brother, wagging a finger at me. "You get an ounce of lead in you and all of a sudden you've grown very smart."

I do not recall that we ever joked together like that before the uprising. Even though he was my brother, he had been my teacher then, and I had been shy and in awe of him. Now it was quite different. I do not know whether, in his eyes, I had grown up or if he had grown closer to me. I only know that nothing does you more good at a bad time than a smile and a little joking.

About ten minutes later, when the moon vanished again behind a cloud, our little caravan quietly pulled out from the beleaguered encampment and quickly headed north, almost following the very trail left by our camels the day before.

My brother and I led the way (he had both arms round me and was propping me up), followed by Bai Nestor and Lilliah. El Shakhin brought up the rear on his horse, and led the other two camels, while Balyu darted back and forth along the line.

We safely navigated the downward slope of the hill and were about to take cover behind the nearby dunes and rocks when a terrible long-drawn wail, like the sound of a cracked zourla, rent the air.

"What's happened?" my brother asked, turning round.

"The yellow camel has tripped," replied El Shakhin in a whisper. "It looks as if its leg . . ."

"Confound it! Now they'll find us. Ride for all you're worth . . ."

Before he had even finished his sentence, shouts echoed throughout the length and breadth of the desert.

"The giaours are getting away!"

"Catch them!"

"They're heading north!"

Now, there was no escape.

"Sorry, Rali," said my brother in a tone of voice I had not heard before, and thrust the revolver into my good hand. "Hold it, boy! Hold it! We'll give them a run for their money."

We sped towards the scattering of rocks where the dunes began. Behind us the thud of horses' hoofs, instead of receding, came nearer and nearer. The thought that we should not be riding two to a camel, flashed through my mind. I turned in the saddle, ducked under my brother's elbow and prepared to shoot, using my left hand.

"Wait till we're past the rocks!" cried Lukan, lashing at the camel.

When we were level with the rocks and I was able to shoot, El Shakhin overtook us on his horse and barred our way.

"Turn off to the left!" he shouted. "Hide over there, Bai Nestor, over there! I'll lure them away!"

We did not know what he had in mind and there was no time to ask. We slipped behind the rocks. If we were going to die, what difference did it make whether it would be here or a little further on?

"What about El Shakhin? Where had he got to?"

At that very minute the Syrian leapt from his saddle. He did not come over to us as I had expected. He seemed to be brandishing some object at the hindquarters of each of the camels in turn, then at the horse. Was he driving them away, whipping them? I do not know. But I have never heard more harrowing sounds than those that reached my ears then. The bellowing of camels, the neighing of a horse—eeee-eah!! The rocks echoed with the sound. A moment later the three animals, wild with pain, hurtled away at such speed that I had no idea where they went.

"A moment later," I say. But that moment gave El Shakhin time to fling himself against the rock. It was well that he did, for just then the zaptiehs came flashing by, yelling and shooting.

"They can chase after us till morning," muttered the Syrian through clenched teeth, slowly wiping the sweat from his brow.

Motionless, we listened to the sound of hoofs receding further and further into the distance.

Finally my brother spoke. "We shan't attempt to thank you, El Shakhin. Words aren't enough. All I shall say is this, that we freed you from your chains, it's true, but you saved our lives. Well, south again!" he added, and I saw him give us an encouraging smile.

In fact, that was all there was left for us to do—encourage one another. We no longer had enough camels to go around.

Chapter 15

Water! Water!

BEFORE THE HOOFBEATS OF THE DEPARTING zaptiehs had died away, I felt the earlier weakness coming over me again. Was it due to loss of blood or to the tension I had gone through? The dark desert swayed before my eyes. There was a steady, high-pitched buzzing in my ears. I began to droop and might have tumbled from the camel if my brother's strong arms had not been there. He pulled me up, hugged me to him and gave me an affectionate pat.

"What is it, Rali?" he asked.

"Nothing. It's all right, Bate. Give the order to start."

"Is it very painful?"

"I don't know. I feel dizzy."

"Give him a sip of water, Lukan," Bai Nestor called from his camel.

"Don't you have the waterskin?"

"I thought you had packed it."

We all—even I, who was barely conscious in my weak state—looked from one to the other, afraid to utter the terrible words. The skin had been left on the yellow camel. We hadn't a single drop of water!

"Oh, we'll manage somehow," said my brother reassuringly. "We are sure to come across a spring."

"There is no water to the south," commented El Shakhin, who was trying to adjust the bridle of Bai Nestor's camel in the dark.

"Do you know these parts?"

"No, I don't, arkadash.* I can't tell you myself."

"What do you mean? I don't understand you, El Shakhin."

"Allah alone knows. One minute I think I have seen these rocks before; then I think that maybe these weren't the ones after all."

"Then why do you tell us that we shan't find a spring?"

"Because I grew up in the desert, and the desert to the south is even more dreadful than this."

More dreadful than this! I could not imagine a region more barren and lifeless than the desert that surrounded us that night. I expected my brother to say something, but he was silent. El Shakhin said nothing more. I wondered what was going on in their minds. Were they thinking up some plan?

"But we can't stay here!" Bai Nestor suddenly exclaimed.

"Let's go," said my brother. "But we won't travel south, we'll go west. That way at least we'll know that we are going towards the sea and not deeper into the desert. What do you say, El Shakhin?"

"West is better, arkadashlar. I've heard that from Chebrisa onwards there are no roads going west, but with luck there may be some water."

So we set off, using the stars to guide us, but whether we were really going west or in some other direction none of us could say for sure. Least of all I, for soon I was nodding to the swaying of the camel and, overcome with a strange lassitude, fell asleep or, rather, lost consciousness. I was aroused only by the sharp hot rays of the sun the next morning. I opened my eyes and looked around me.

We were traveling over wild, stony terrain, and its most striking feature was the rocks. They were not round and sandy like the others but sharp, like thin slices of slate. They evidently contained scales of some glistening substance, because they gave off a dazzling sparkle and seemed to light up the surrounding landscape with their innumerable reflections.

I turned around and discovered that my brother was not riding behind me. He had tied me to the saddle and was walking beside the camel. Bai Nestor was walking beside the other camel, on which Lilliah slept with her head resting on its hump. El Shakhin was nowhere to be seen.

Memories of the search party, of the battle and our flight came crowding into my mind. I had been wounded. Was it serious? Was I going to die, I wondered anxiously, but in a somewhat detached way, as if the problem did not concern me.

Actually, from the moment that the fifty screaming zaptiehs had come storming towards my position, my memories became blurred. The bullet had entered my shoulder from the front, and had certainly penetrated the shoulder blade, I seemed to recall. But hadn't I felt a pain somewhere else just before that? In my right heel, or a little higher up? It still felt sore there. I sat up and looked at my foot. It had been securely bandaged with a piece of cloth. Nothing much. It would heal like that injury I received in Panagyurishte, I told myself. But I could not help wondering how I had been hit so low down. Hadn't I been hiding behind the rocks? Then the bullet must have ricocheted, I reasoned, whereas in the shoulder I had received a direct hit. Why had Lukan made that joke about an ounce of lead, I suddenly thought. If the bullet is still inside me, then things are really bad! Again I thought that perhaps I would die, pictured my brother and Lilliah, Bai Nestor and El Shakhin, all weeping over my grave, and felt very sorry for myself.

The thought of the Syrian reminded me that I had not seen him. I looked round again.

"Where is El Shakhin?" I asked aloud.

"So you are awake, Rali. Have you had a good sleep?" my brother asked, instead of answering my question and, stretching out a hand, patted my head. "How do you feel now? Do your wounds hurt?"

"I'm thirsty," I said. "Can I have a sip of water?"

> 171

"Water. . . ."

I noticed that he licked his lips and swallowed. But, as usual, he did not betray any emotion. He smiled and said, "Be patient, boy. El Shakhin has gone to find some."

He had barely uttered the last few words when I recollected, to my horror, that the skin had been left behind on the yellow camel and that we had not a single drop of water.

"Where did El Shakhin go? How long ago?" I asked in a husky voice.

"He . . . he's somewhere around here, Rali. He's exploring all the hollows in the area. If he finds water, he'll call us."

"But what if he loses us?"

"Balyu is with him."

I closed my eyes. El Shakhin was exploring the hollows. What water could he find among these glittering rocks?

No, this is the way we shall die, I thought, feeble with exhaustion and thirst. I shall be the first to go, as I am badly wounded anyway. Then it will be Lilliah's turn because she is a woman and won't have the strength to survive, and after that it will be Bai Nestor. I almost took a strange perverse pleasure in contemplating the dreadful fate that awaited us. But when I came to my brother and El Shakhin, I could not decide which of them would succumb first. They both seemed equally hardy. The Syrian was sturdy and tough, used to the desert; Lukan was a stubborn, strong-willed person who, as long as he had a breath in his body, would never lose heart or give up. Besides, although I could easily imagine my own death, for some reason I simply could not admit that my brother could die like everyone else. But why brood over these foolish fantasies, I kept telling myself. Had it been any easier in Diyarbakir? Think of all the trials and troubles we surmounted there. But at Diyarbakir we had been up against people, and walls built by people. Whereas here, whichever way you turned, there was always the same thin desert grass, the same grating sand—we were covered with it—and the same glistening rocks. Without water we would perish, we *were* perishing! And the sun—there it was, a blaze of orange, filling half the sky.

We traveled for another hour, or perhaps two; then suddenly I heard Balyu's bark, followed by the sound of El Shakhin's voice.

"No luck," he said.

"Perhaps a little further on?" suggested my brother.

"I have been over the whole area."

"What about that hill over there?"

"I have been there too. There's nothing. Besides, I know those shiny rocks drink up all the water around."

They stopped talking and I did not even look to see if El Shakhin went off again in search of a life-saving spring. I lay curled up in the saddle on the camel which was rocking like a ship at sea. I gazed into the distance, listening to the throbbing of the inflamed wound in my shoulder, groaning faintly at regular intervals and thinking only that I was thirsty and that nothing could be more welcome than a few gulps of water.

Lilliah, on the other camel, made some remark to her father. My brother joined in their conversation and, as he was walking close beside me, I heard him reassure her:

"Just don't think about it, Lilliah! If we find some, you and Rali will be the first to have a drink."

How long will it be? How long will we last? In my drowsy state I kept repeating these questions to myself and hours must have gone by, for I became aware suddenly that El

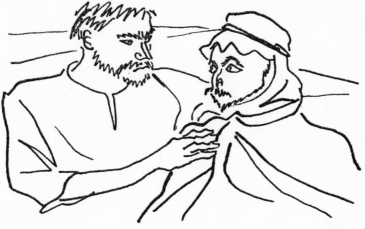

Shakhin was back again. His little bony face appeared near me. It was now so thin and so caked with sand that I scarcely recognized it.

"There is none there either," he told my brother.

I did not know what place they were talking about, but they were saying that there was no water, and that was enough for me.

We stopped several times to rest and, by the time lunch was over (I ate a rusk and some olives, which seemed to make me twice as thirsty), both humans and camels could barely drag themselves along.

"This is where we are going to die, fellows, right here!" Bai Nestor groaned in despair at one point. "Never mind about me, but think of Lilliah and Rali, and you too, Lukan. Ooooh!"

It was fortunate that he spoke in Bulgarian, so that only my brother and I understood. It would have been too much for Lilliah, whose eyes wandered imploringly from her father to my brother, as if looking for help.

"People who have survived a dungeon, as we have, don't talk about death, Bai Nestor," said my brother.

"What are you saying? I can't understand a word. Don't keep things from me," Lilliah said and unaccountably burst into tears.

I was amazed. She did not know what they were talking about; yet she was crying. In some way I could not understand she sensed the meaning of the words. Alas! There was no hope. As far as the eye could see, nothing but these sharp rocks, scattered over the desert. . . . My eye wandered to the horizon and I caught my breath in amazement.

"Look!" I cried, raising up in the saddle. "We're saved! We're saved!"

I felt a stab of pain in my shoulder, but I was so wild with joy that I stretched out my injured arm and pointed to the horizon, shouting, "Look! Look!"

"What do you see?"

"What is it, Rali?"

"Trees . . . water!" I shouted hoarsely.

Indeed, just above the craggy horizon a green oasis was

clearly outlined in the shimmering haze of the afternoon. A little limpid pool, shaded by clusters of palm trees and surrounded by dumpy white houses, with camels going for a drink.

"We're saved! We're saved!" shouted Lilliah, Bai Nestor and Lukan in unison. Even Balyu began to bark and wag his tail for joy.

"Quick! Turn the camels around," ordered my brother. "In two hours we'll be there. El Shakhin, why are you standing there like that? Why don't you move?"

"What is the matter with you, man?" I heard Bai Nestor say.

I managed to tear my eyes from the sight we had so longed to see, turned round and looked at the Syrian. He was standing apart from us, his hands hanging loosely by his sides, his head drooping. In all the time I had known him I had never seen him so dejected.

"There is no oasis there," he said quietly.

"You're crazy!" shrieked Bai Nestor, beside himself.

El Shakhin shook his head. "There is no oasis, I say."

"What is wrong with you, man? Can't you see?"

"I can see," our friend mumbled unhappily. "That is a mirage, arkadashlar. It's an optical illusion. It will disappear in a minute. There! You see?"

We turned, as one to the horizon, but we were not quick enough. There, where the palm trees, the pool and the signs of life had been, was nothing but bare, white-hot, shimmering sky.

"Ooooh!" wailed Lilliah, her whole body shaking with sobs.

Her father, my brother and even El Shakhin turned to comfort her. I don't know how it happened, but all at once my whole outlook changed. It's no use crying over spilt milk, I told myself. We are responsible for our own fate. The longer we delay, the more difficult we make things for ourselves.

"Listen, everyone, don't let's stop, let's keep moving," I cried. "If that is a mirage, it must mean that somewhere there really is a pool, with palm trees and everything."

This speech was so unexpected that Lilliah stopped crying.

She looked at me through her long lashes, then at my brother, who was nearest to her, and smiled at him.

Her smile found its way to his face.

"Come on, spur the camels," he said, flushed with excitement. "And how about singing a song, eh?"

Before any of us could reply, he started singing at the top of his voice. It was the song of the exiles, which I had heard many times before, wafting faintly and tunelessly from the dark dungeons in the fortress of Diyarbakir:

> Oh how painful and how wrong
> In a foreign land to toil.
> Pleasant homeland, how I long
> To die on your sweet soil...

The rest of us took up the refrain, weeping as we sang. After that we sang two more songs, in which both Lilliah and El Shakhin joined. Our blackest despair had turned, in a moment, to unaccountable and unexpected elation that saved us. As it happened, we did not find water that day. Nor the next. Nor the following night. But somehow or other we did not lose heart. Before sunrise of the third morning, after holding a consultation with my brother and Bai Nestor, the Syrian led off Lilliah's camel somewhere behind the rocks. Later he returned without it, carefully carrying a large water bottle in each hand.

"There," he said, handing them to my brother. "Now, how about the meat?"

My brother shrugged his shoulders and looked uncomfortable. "We still have some rusks and olives."

"It's eatable. It's just a bit tough," insisted El Shakhin.

"Do as you think best. Lilliah! Rali! Here's some water!"

"Water?" the girl jumped up, her large eyes wide with amazement.

I merely put out a hand and seized the other bottle.

"A little each," cautioned Lukan. "Five swallows each, no more. We have a long journey ahead."

I paid no attention. I just couldn't. The liquid filled my mouth and flowed through my whole body.

"That's enough, Rali," said my brother, snatching the bottle from my hands.

"Another drop. Oh, please, please!"

"No, young man, not till lunchtime."

A similar conversation was going on nearby between Bai Nestor and his daughter.

"We'll have a sip, too, shall we? Three swallows each," Lukan said, turning to the old man and El Shakhin.

"I've had some," replied the Syrian.

He left us and disappeared again behind the rocks. I remembered that they had talked about some meat and imagined that he was going to get it now. I realized why he had taken the camel away and where he had got the water. I was amazed that it had taken me so long to think of it. Abu Talib had once told me that each of these animals had a place in its body where it stored spare water, something like a tank. So El Shakhin had slaughtered the camel. The water came from its belly! Oh, no, don't imagine that the thought turned my stomach! Well, as a matter of fact it did upset me, but only in theory. My eyes were riveted on the bottle that my brother was corking so carefully. I could easily have drunk another hundred mouthfuls!

"Give Balyu some too," I pleaded. "Look, his tongue is hanging out and he can hardly breathe."

Without a word Lukan poured a little water into the hollow of my hand and I offered it to my dog. He made such a wild lunge at my hand that I thought he would gobble it up.

"We now have enough water for two more rounds like that," said my brother.

"What about the water in my camel?"

He gave me a sharp look; then his face softened. "We'd better not think about that, Rali. If we are left without your camel, how will we carry you? Lilliah will join you up there now," he added.

"I'll walk," she said when she realized what we were talking about.

"No, Lilliah, if you walk you will wear yourself out. Ride with Rali."

He lifted me up and set me in the saddle of the kneeling

camel. Then he helped the girl up behind me. On looking round, I noticed a bright flush in their thin cheeks.

And I was not the only one who saw this and understood. El Shakhin, who was silently approaching with a bundle in his arms, also noticed. He dropped his eyes and quickly crept away. Did the two of them sense that we had guessed their secret, I wondered, trembling with excitement. I suspect they did not. They probably thought that it was carefully hidden from all but themselves. Or, more likely still, they thought nothing at all—who knows? I was too young to appreciate all the finer shades of the feeling that was growing up between them day by day, in spite of all the privations and hardships.

The next two days brought no new developments. We encountered neither an oasis nor a spring, nor any deep depression that could hold water. However, the rocks were replaced by arid steppe. That in itself was a sign of better things to come, because our camel would stop to munch the tough, prickly clumps of thorn that dotted the steppe, or nibble at the roots as if it could smell water somewhere underneath.

I said "smell water," which may sound fanciful or absurd to some. Yet it is perfectly true. Somehow that smell could be detected not just in the ground but in the very air. If a west wind was blowing, we would automatically stop, lift our emaciated weather-beaten faces and sniff, like Balyu and the camel. And, like them, we would catch the indefinable, fresh, familiar smell of water.

Where was it? It would be foolish to suppose that it came from the sea, for that was still hundreds and hundreds of miles away. Then there must be a vast expanse of forest somewhere ahead. A forest in the steppe? Impossible! Or perhaps there was water in some dark, hidden recess in the mountains. However, as far as the eye could see there was no sign of a mountain.

On the third day, when we were again overcome with unbearable thirst and torn between hope and despair, El Shakhin suddenly uttered a strange inarticulate cry, waved his arm like a lunatic, then sank to his knees and raised his hands in prayer.

"Allah akbar!"* he cried, prostrating himself on the ground.

"What is it, El Shakhin? Tell us, tell us, don't keep us in suspense!" My brother rushed up to him, with Bai Nestor and Lilliah, who had got off the camel in order to stretch her legs.

"Water, brothers! Water!"

Lukan looked up and scanned the horizon with feverish eyes. I, too, gazed into the distance but, as hard as I peered, I could see nothing.

"I don't understand," sighed Lukan. "There's nothing there."

"Tell us, good El Shakhin, tell us where the water is," pleaded Lilliah, her eyes bright with hope and so excited that she was shaking the kneeling Syrian by the shoulders.

El Shakhin trembled from head to foot, his face shone with an inner light and his expression was proud and triumphant.

Suddenly his face clouded over, the triumphant light faded. He sprang to his feet and pointed.

"Do you see that white vapor over there?" Although he spoke to all of us, I had the impression that he was addressing Lilliah particularly.

"It is probably haze," said Bai Nestor, screwing up his eyes.

"No, arkadashlar, it's vapor."

"But from what?"

"Do you think it's a lake?" I asked.

"Not a lake, a large river. My river, Father Euphrates!"

"Father Euphrates?" I repeated, and suddenly remembered Abu Talib saying that name. He had not misled me. At last, Father Euphrates was in sight!

Chapter 16

Kyr Lambros of Rakka and his friend, Doctor Judah ben Ephraim

I SHALL SAY NO MORE OF OUR HURRIED JOURNEY towards the great river, than that we drank there insatiably until we felt quite ill and had to lie on the bank for hours, still unable to believe that we had been saved from dying of thirst.

When we all had recovered, my brother sent El Shakhin to spy out the land along the river. He headed north and came back an hour later, his face radiant.

"We're in luck," he announced. "I saw the minarets of a town. If we hurry, we may get there before nightfall."

The town our friend had discovered was called Rakka. It was not far away, but we felt so tired that, by the time the great hot sun had sunk halfway into the waters of the Euphrates and, for a moment, the sky was a blaze of red and gold, we had only just reached the harbor. This was outside and a little to one side of the city walls of Rakka.

I remember that this harbor, though not large, struck me as being full of life. Its open yards were cluttered with tumble-down wooden shacks and round clay huts. By the two wharfs and all along the riverbank, there were dozens of boats, double boats of a kind I had never seen before, as well as ordinary narrow boats and others that were circular, like huge baskets coated with pitch. The fishermen had just come back from the day's work and the afternoon air rang with their shouts and laughter. Apparently all these noisy people lived not in the town but in the shacks and tumble-down houses by the water. We, therefore, felt safe immediately, and the only thing we had to be careful about was not revealing who we were or where we came from.

We all agreed that the task of finding food and lodging for the night should fall, once again, to the invaluable El Shakhin who, being an Arab, was the least likely to arouse suspicion. Indeed he accomplished it so swiftly and so successfully that half an hour later we had rented—with Hadji Doino's money—one of the harbor buildings, a hut made of plaited sticks and covered with palm leaves. It belonged to a merchant named Kyr Lambros, who promptly paid us a visit that same evening.

The Greek arrived just as we were having supper. I was lying on a pile of my brother's clothes beside the snorting camel, convulsed with spasms of pain from the wound in my shoulder. I have no idea what I was thinking about, but I remember that I caught sight of Lilliah's face in the candlelight and noticed that her eyes were fastened on the door of the hut. It was more from her expression of alarm than from the faint creak of the door that I realized that someone had entered.

"Aha! You are having supper?" said an ingratiating voice. "Carry on! Don't let me disturb you," he continued in Turkish instead of Arabic.

I lifted my head and looked at the visitor. The light from the lantern he carried showed me a shortish middle-aged man with a flat bony head and mustaches that curled like the horns of a ram. He stood with his head slightly inclined, as if he were on the alert for some reason, and bared all his yellow, decaying teeth in an unctuous smile while his deep-set eyes roved over us.

"Thank you," said Bai Nestor. Whereupon Lukan began to question him.

"Who are you? What do you want?"

"Who am I? Well, that friend of yours over there will tell you who I am. You were the one who came to see me, weren't you, my dear sir?" said the visitor, approaching the Syrian with a polite bow.

"This gentleman is the owner of the hut, arkadashlar," explained El Shakhin. "Kyr* Lambros, these are the friends I told you about."

"Ah, how nice, how nice to see such fine company! I am so, so happy."

"We thank you for giving us shelter, dear kyrie," said my brother, about to rise. Having once studied in Russia, he was particular about good manners.

The Greek stopped him quickly. "Be seated, be seated, my dear sir. Dear me, how tired you must be! And why, oh why, should you thank me? I have a hut, so naturally I let you have it. Why shouldn't I?"

There was certainly no reason why he should not let us have it, since El Shakhin had paid him a whole lira for us to spend the night there. He was obviously a shrewd and rapacious man, that much we saw—but the worst was yet to come!

"Is there anything else you need? You have had a journey, but I shall not ask where you have come from. Heaven preserve me! Everyone has the right to travel the wide world. But you need mattresses. Yes, I'll rent you some mattresses for only two piasters apiece. Goodness, if you went to an inn! God forbid! At an inn they would charge you at least five piasters, my dear friends. Oh, no! And then they would start asking, 'Where are you from? Where are you going? Where are your papers?' "

"Our friend probably told you that we were attacked by bandits and they robbed us of everything."

"I know, I know! May God strike those bandits dead! What a good thing they left you your money!"

"We managed to hide something, Kyr Lambros."

"What a good thing you did! Where would you be without money? Look at me, I've always been ready to do a good deed, and yet . . . oh, yes, there are bad people in these parts. Ugh, such bad people! So you'll take five mattresses?"

"No, two will be enough," said my brother.

I knew that he thoroughly detested wily people of this kind, but he had to put up with it. What else could he do?

"Oh well, if you say two, two it shall be," the merchant said, smiling. "And what about blankets? Do you have any blankets? You haven't! It gets cold here at night, my dear sirs. The river . . . I'm sure you have no idea what the river is like! Besides, you have a young woman with you, and a boy. Is he ill! Earlier, when I looked out from my shop, I had the impression he was ill."

"We can manage without blankets," put in Bai Nestor. "We are used to it by now."

"Without blankets? Oh, my dear, good sir! How can you possibly manage? I must say, if you were at an inn . . . but I charge so little, a purely nominal sum, three piasters a blanket. No, I'll only charge two. Just for you!"

"Very well, send along two blankets as well," my brother broke in with a frown of displeasure. "And, thank you, we don't need anything else."

"I'll arrange it right away, my dear sir! I am happy to be of service to you. A friend in need is a friend indeed! Oh yes! But what is the matter with this boy!"

He bent over me and in the semi-darkness I saw a gleam in his eyes as he looked me over.

"Well, well! What a fine boy! What did you say was wrong with him?"

"Nothing. He's not feeling himself, that's all."

"Ooh!" he exclaimed, suddenly running his hand over my forehead. "He's feverish! You must go to the doctor! And what is this? Is he wounded? And in the leg, too?"

I threw an appealing glance at my brother, but he was bristling with indignation, and looked as if at any moment he might pounce on the merchant and seize him by the throat.

"There is nothing the matter with me," I said, but my weak voice gave me away. I glared angrily at the Greek.

"He was wounded by the bandits," said my brother curtly.

"Oh, what bad people there are about! What wicked people!

And to think that my boat sails down the Euphrates with all that merchandise. Goodness! It's sailing again tomorrow evening. What a thought! Is he badly wounded?"

"No . . . that is . . . where is the doctor?" my brother asked suddenly.

"Ah, there! I knew it! The doctor, my esteemed friend Judah ben Ephraim, is now in the town and is probably dining with his children and grandchildren, my dear sir. Yes, yes, he is there now and if you would like to visit him at his home, you will pay exactly one gold lira."

"Surely the gates of the town are closed in the evening. How will we get in?"

"Ah, yes! Of course they are closed! But if, in addition to the gold lira for my honorable friend, you give me another half lira, perhaps the gates will be opened for you. That is how things are in our town of Rakka, my dear, that is the kind of town we have."

"No. We'll wait till sunrise."

"Tomorrow it may be too late." The Greek shook his head.

"I can't move my brother just like that, Kyr Lambros! No, let's hope that nothing will happen. We'll send for your friend first thing in the morning!"

Lukan clearly did not want to risk entering the town at night when any wretch of a zaptieh could ask us for papers which, needless to say, we did not have.

"But why tomorrow? Why not now? And if you contribute another small sum, that is, if you make it exactly three liras, dear sir, in a very short time my friend Judah ben Ephraim will be here."

Oh, what an extortioner the man was! I signaled to my brother that he should agree, but he did not even look at me.

"Send for him," Lukan said, standing up.

"But the money,"—the Greek squirmed—"leave the money with me as a deposit and I'll send for the doctor."

There was no alternative. Lukan took out three liras and gave them to him.

Doctor Judah ben Ephraim, a little wizened, bearded old man, wearing a fur hat and a worn caftan and carrying a large basket, arrived about midnight. He was accompanied by a plump, indolent servant. Since Kyr Lambros was not there to confirm that the doctor had received the money for the treatment, my brother hastily said, "Please take out the bullet, doctor. You will be paid. If necessary we shall pay extra."

"For extracting a bullet I am paid five piasters," said the old man shortly. "Two piasters for the poor, two for the synagogue and one for me, that shall be your fee, my children."

We exchanged glances. Five piasters! And that wily Greek had gone off with three liras, that is, three hundred piasters! Where was he? No doubt fast asleep, the barefaced robber!

"Is this the patient? What is the matter, son, is it very painful?" The old Jew knelt down beside me and I don't know whether it was on account of his voice or what he said, but I felt complete confidence in him.

"Bring the lantern over here," he ordered, and started to unbandage my shoulder. "What are you? You aren't Turkish, are you?"

"Ouch!" I exclaimed. The blood-soaked bandage had stuck to my skin and the wound opened when he pulled it off.

Another groan sounded in the dark hut and I heard my brother say, "Take her outside, Bai Nestor."

Why should they take Lilliah outside? Ah well, perhaps it was better that way, so that she would not see, I reasoned in my fevered mind as the firm, bony fingers of the doctor probed,

pulled and squeezed. I caught my breath and felt as if I would scream, and perhaps I did. I only know that the pain was terrible, more than I could bear.

"Just a little longer, young man! Hold out a little longer!" Lukan kept repeating in a whisper, bending over me from the other side.

His strong arms had me pinned to the mattress, and when, in a spasm of pain my head twisted round in his direction, I saw tears glistening in his eyes.

"Oh, Bate, ooh!" I groaned.

"Just a little longer, just a little . . ."

Suddenly I felt a sharp stab in my shoulder. Red and black circles danced before my eyes.

"Aaah! It hurts!" I yelled and struggled so violently that I escaped my brother's grasp.

"It's all over, lad. There it is, it's out," I heard the gentle old voice say. The doctor was holding up a pair of bloody forceps, their pincers gripping a tiny fragment of flattened lead.

What—that? Could that tiny fragment have caused all that pain? I could not believe it. The doctor put away the forceps and the piece of bullet.

"Now hold still a little longer," he said, "so that I can clean out the wound. I'll dress it with my ointments and, God willing, everything will be all right, young fellow."

Compared with the pain I had endured, the discomfort of having the wound washed and dressed was nothing.

"Will it heal soon?" I asked, half fearful, half hopeful.

"Everything will be all right. Don't worry. Just lie there and rest. And eat as much as you can. You need to get your strength back now. What is your name?"

His question was so unexpected that neither I nor my brother was prepared for it. Should I give my assumed name, Ali? But why lie? Why continue to conceal my real name, especially from this kind, gentle old doctor. After all, the search party was miles away!

"My name is Rali, sir!" I replied boldly.

"Rali? That's a foreign name. Now, I'm going to bandage you up, Rali. Tomorrow evening, when I come, I shall put some more ointment on your wound. And again the next day. And, God willing, the day after that. Yes, yes, everything will be all right. Life is for the young, and we old ones should be on our way. That's it, young fellow, that's it," the doctor reflected aloud, with a kindly twinkle in his dark, close-set eyes that were as faded as his robe.

"So, now I can be going."

But my brother stopped him.

"He, Rali, has another injury. It's nothing much, but please dress it too."

"Of course, I'll dress it. Where is it, my boy? Will you show it to me?"

I lifted up my leg and Lukan hastened to unbind it.

The doctor lowered the lantern, bent down and examined the injury. I thought he spent more time looking at it than he had inspecting my inflamed shoulder. Then he raised his head and thoughtfully stroked his yellowing beard.

"What is it?" I asked impatiently.

"Nothing, lad. This will heal too. Only it will take time. Ointment will not cure that injury."

"What? Is it bad?" my brother and I exclaimed at the same time.

"No, it's not that bad. But it's not good either, lads. It's a tendon. Do you know what that is? It's torn. But in a month's time . . ."

"A month!"

"Well, maybe a little less, maybe even longer. It will mend, you are young, Rali. Your name is Rali, isn't it? I forget."

I nodded, but my thoughts were far from cheerful. A month, two months, all for that silly tendon! And to think that all that time I'd be a burden to the others. If only it were for the sake of a real wound, but for this trifle that I hadn't even bothered about!

The doctor washed the entire lower part of my leg, bandaged it securely and got up to go. Bowing his thanks, my brother silently offered him a lira.

"No," the old man said and put his hand behind him. "That is not what we agreed. The fee is five piasters—two for the poor, two for the synagogue and one for me." He was so firm that it was useless for us to try to persuade him to take more.

"Well, then, we thank you from the bottom of our hearts," said Lukan.

"What have I done, children? I have done nothing. Youth is doing it all," said the doctor. He nodded to Bai Nestor, who had come back into the hut with Lilliah, and to El Shakhin, who was standing in the shadows, and said, "To-morrow evening I shall come again." Then he turned to leave, accompanied by the servant who had been dozing by the door all that time and had just waked up.

I propped myself up on my good arm and gazed after the little old man, who left as quietly and unobtrusively as he had arrived.

"I thank you too, Doctor Judah ben Ephraim," I whispered. But my heart was unspeakably heavy, because the thought of dragging about on a lame leg for months to come could scarcely have been more intolerable to anyone than to me.

That night I dreamt of Abu Talib.

It was a strange dream that I had. By some inexplicable means the doctor Judah ben Ephraim and the innkeeper from Diyarbakir had become the same person. He was called Abu Talib, but he was a diminutive Abu Talib with the faded moist eyes of the old Jew and the same gentle voice. He was an-nointing me with his ointments, but instead of real ointments they were food, watery concoctions swimming in fat. I am not sure whether I had any wounds or not. We were at his inn, I distinctly remember. The same inn except that the walls were made of shiny glittering slate, like the rocks that had been all around us in the desert. I was startled by the sound of gruff voices. I looked round and, from the recess where we were conversing in undertones, I saw the serving-counter and sickly Yakub, the servant, handing round a large tray of coffee to the agalar of Diyarbakir. Wasn't that Hadji Hassan with the blue nose? And that other one, with the melancholy face, surely it was the town clerk. But where was his newspaper, why had he no paper? Who was that large stout man with the overbearing manner? With a shudder of horror I realized that was Feisal Bey! He held a pistol in one hand and a yataghan in the other. Although he was shouting at the top of his voice, I could not hear a thing, but I distinctly heard Abu Talib whisper, "They've found out, Ali. That is why they are meeting."

"They know everything? Who gave me away?"

"Toparlak Bekir could have said something. After all, he knows you," suggested Abu Talib.

"The eunuch? I don't believe it."

"I don't say it was he. But he could have said something to . . ."

"Oh, he never seemed that bad! Surely someone who sings can't have evil designs, dear Abu Talib. And Toparlak Bekir used to sing, I remember. Shall I sing you his song?" I started to sing the song that I found so easy to memorize: "Oooo . . . o . . . Eeee . . . e!"

"So that is the way Toparlak Bekir used to sing!" The transfigured Abu Talib shook his head and regarded me steadily with his faded, close-set eyes. "Don't believe it, son! Allah has said that any man born of woman has some evil in him."

"No, that's not true! You're not bad! You helped my brother and me to escape. You helped me in everything! You were like a father to me and I was like your son. You told me so yourself!"

Suddenly a sneer appeared on the gentle face of the diminutive Abu Talib.

All of a sudden, Abu Talib reassumed his normal features. He had a jutting beard and had grown to an incredible height. In fact, he no longer bore the slightest resemblance to the little doctor.

"So, what is your name?" he asked, looking down at me. "What is your real name? Will you tell me?"

"Rali!"

"Well, well! A clever dodge, Rali-Ali! Are you a Moslem?"

"I am a Christian."

"Hm! I see."

"Why should that bother you, Abu Talib?"

"And your nationality? Are you a Turk?"

"I am a Bulgarian."

"A Bulgarian, one of those trouble-makers! This war that has broken out is all because of you people."

"It's to rid us of eternal bondage, dear Abu Talib. You have no idea! They killed my father. And my mother and Petra—my grandmother, too—they were burnt to death. Our house was destroyed . . . the whole town. I must tell you the whole story! You are sure to understand if I tell you."

"Don't shout," he said. "Feisal Bey is out to get you anyway! He lost two slaves on account of you. If he finds out that you are the one . . ."

"He won't find out unless you tell him, Abu Talib! And you will keep quiet, won't you? Tell me, it *was* someone else who betrayed me, wasn't it?"

He made no reply and I tried to look him in the eye but his face was too far above mine and, although I tried standing on tiptoe, his neck grew longer and longer, and I could not see into his eyes.

"Oh dear! Oh dear!" A wail arose from the huddle of agalar.

Feisal Bey thundered in a terrible voice, "Yakub, put down the coffee! Tell me at once, was it you they were telling me about? Are you the giaour?"

"Who told you, bey effendi?" I spoke up from my corner.

"Ah, so it wasn't Yakub. It was that boy who was posing as a boza-seller. Seize him, seize him!"

"Seize him!" chorused the Turks. But, for some reason, none of them stirred from their places. Only the melancholy town clerk with the drooping nose suddenly appeared, for no apparent reason, behind the serving-counter and started singing in a mournful wail:

> There are none stronger than us,
> None more glorious than us! . . .

"Russia is stronger!" I shouted.

Someone grabbed me from behind and tried to muzzle me, but I kept shouting at the top of my voice.

"Russia is stronger!"

"What is it, Rali? What are you shouting for?"

I woke up. My brother and Lilliah were bending over me. It was light inside the hut.

"Oh," I gasped, "I was dreaming." I wanted to tell him about my dream but he stood up.

"When we come back, Rali. We're in a hurry now. Bai Nestor is here. He's outside in front of the hut. If you need anything, just shout."

"Where are you going?"

"I'm going with Lilliah to buy a few things. We have to prepare for the journey. We can't stay here for ever. The search party is after us and it might turn up at any minute!"

"The search party?"

I remembered my dream. Feisal Bey flourishing his pistol and sword and screaming at me. Then there was Abu Talib. Oh, what a dream! What unworthy thoughts about my benefactor!

"I don't see El Shakhin," I said.

"He went out an hour ago. He's going to try to slip into town. We have to find out if they know anything about us yet."

"Good. Then you'd better go too," I urged. "Last night I saw them selling oranges by the wharfs. Buy me one if you can, Bate. I have such a craving for one."

My brother nodded. Lilliah smiled at me and they started towards the door. I could see that they were eager to be alone.

Well, what was surprising about that? It was obvious that they had eyes only for each other.

They went out. The door closed behind them and I lay there for a long time wondering where they were going and what they would see. I felt a sharp pang of loneliness. But was I really alone in the hut! Ridiculous! There was Balyu curled up at my feet. Balyu, my faithful friend through thick and thin! I called him and he promptly got up, shook himself and nuzzled my face, with a happy whimper.

"Dear old pal," I murmured, stroking his head with my good hand.

"Lie down, lie down here. That's it. Stay and have a chat. We've covered some distance and been through some hard times, you and I. I haven't forgotten, Balyu. Remember that time when I was leaving Panagyurishte and turned to look back? There you were following me, just you. And the time outside the prison at Plovdiv, and those nights on the journey when we would creep up to see Lukan. And the time I was ill, do you remember? If you hadn't kept me warm in that rain, and if you hadn't kept me company, I would have died, Balyu! Nobody knows, nobody, not even Lukan knows, what you've been to me!"

I went on recounting the narrow escapes and the adventures we had had, while Balyu licked my hand and face and regarded me with his faithful, intelligent eyes. "Oh, Balyu, when will we see home again? Oh, to be home!" And for a long, long time, I thought of home.

Bai Nestor came twice into the hut, now flooded with daylight, but I did not speak to him and he went out again, probably thinking I was asleep. He had placed a bottle of water beside me. There was also some food. I ate and drank and gave some to Balyu. Eventually I drifted off to sleep.

I was awakened by the loud slamming of the door.

I looked up. A large, curving object blocked the light. A camel! Not ours, another one. Behind it walked Lukan, followed by Lilliah and her father.

"This one was a real bargain," said Lukan. I was going to buy another, but it seemed too expensive, so I turned it down. We are already halfway through Hadji Doino's money.

We'll have to budget carefully. I bought some rusks and some olives, four waterskins and some dried meat."

"You've forgotten the most important thing of all," Lilliah said with a smile.

"Oh, of course! I bought you a whole basketful of oranges!"

"Bate!" I exclaimed. "You *are* kind! Goodness knows what you must have spent on me! I said only one orange."

"I got a whole basket and a bag of coconuts as well, *and* two bunches of dates—all for twelve piasters, Rali."

"But what will I do with them! I shan't be able to eat all that."

"We'll help you," my brother assured me. "For goodness' sake!" he continued, laughing, "since we've come all the way to Asia, we might, at least, taste its fruits. Go on, help yourselves."

We needed no further prompting. The three sat down beside me and we made such a hearty meal of the fresh, succulent southern fruits that before we knew it we had demolished half the supply.

"We must leave some for El Shakhin," said Lilliah.

"We certainly must," Bai Nestor promptly agreed.

Lukan added, "He will appreciate them more than any of us. This fruit comes from his country."

We discussed what else we needed to buy. Then my brother told of their meeting our landlord, Kyr Lambros. He had been down at the wharf, where his boat was being loaded with merchandise. It was due to sail that night down the river to Ana and Feludjah.

"He rubbed his hands and bowed," Lukan related, half angry and half amused. "I challenged him over the doctor. I asked him why he hadn't given Doctor Judah ben Ephraim the money he had taken from us."

"And what did he say?"

"He promptly replied, 'Everything's settled, my dear sir.'"

"My dear sir! Ha! Ha!" I said.

"Then he exclaimed, 'What! Me cheat my friend? My best friend, Judah ben Ephraim? Didn't you see the kind of man he was? How could I cheat someone like that?'"

"That fellow is a perfect clown, Lukan!"

"Some clown, Bai Nestor! He robbed us of a tidy sum of money and he'll get plenty more out of us yet."

"There's not much we can do about it."

"I should have wrung his neck. You are right, though, he has got us in a tight corner. We'll have to put up with it."

"We'll put up with it. Never mind about the money or anything else, just so long as we get out of here," declared Bai Nestor.

"That's the way I feel, too. I have paid him for tonight as well," Lukan told him.

"Another lira gone!"

Lukan nodded.

"That was nothing. When he saw the money, there was no getting away from him. 'There's no road down the river,' he shouted, 'but there's just room for you in the boat. I'll only charge you two liras a head, and one lira each for the camels.' "

"Robber!" I cried. "Extortioner! Thinks we need his boat, does he?"

"The river is no use to us. We'll cut straight across to the west. We'll keep going as long as we can," Bai Nestor said.

"I'm for that too. If we can just get to the sea!" my brother cried.

"The sea, Lukan, ah, the sea! And beyond the sea, lads, beyond the sea, the mere thought does something to my heart. Twenty years! It's been twenty years since I've seen our native land, boys. And now I'm taking a daughter there."

He turned tear-filled eyes to Lilliah, who was unloading the camel they had brought back.

Just then El Shakhin appeared.

"They are after us!" he cried from the door, flinging down two large sacks, tied together, which he had been carrying over his shoulder like saddle bags.

"Who? Who's after us? Feisal Bey?" we all shouted at once.

"The search party, arkadashlar."

"But how can they be?"

El Shakhin sat down and, before continuing, drank some water out of the bottle.

"Here, have an orange," said Lilliah, holding out the basket to him.

He gave her a quick glance, took one, then looking away, started to tell his story.

"When I left here this morning I went round by the wharfs."

"We went there too," my brother broke in. "Did you get into town?"

"I got in," said the Syrian, deftly and swiftly peeling the orange. "It wasn't easy, but I managed. They are calling up the reservists for the war now, and there are a lot of people going in and out, so I slipped in with them. The town isn't large, but there seems to be plenty of trade. All the roads from the north end here. There is also a road that goes straight to Diyarbakir."

"How come we didn't know about it?" exclaimed Bai Nestor.

"I knew about it," I put in hastily. "But Abu Talib said that they always look for fugitives on the shortest road first."

"That's not an infallible rule," my brother commented wryly. "Since we were taking the longest . . ."

"That was mere chance!"

"Let us hope it was chance, Rali! Go on, El Shakhin. Never mind about Rakka and its trade. We're already well acquainted with one of the local tradesmen. Tell us, did you see Feisal Bey?"

"No, I didn't see him, arkadashlar."

"And what about his men?"

"I didn't see his men either."

"Well then?"

"Well, I was hanging around the coffeehouses and I heard someone say, 'The bey was here three days ago. He told the sentries at the city gates that if they saw a group of escaped infidels, with a boy and a young slave-girl, they were to seize them immediately.' "

"Thank God, we were late last night!" Bai Nestor interjected and crossed himself.

As usual, Lukan's mind was on the most important thing. "Did you find out where Feisal Bey is now?" he asked.

"He went over to the other side of the river with his men.

Evidently he went to alert the villagers there. He is expected back tomorrow."

"That's bad," Bai Nestor observed, shaking his head. "They are cutting off our escape route, fellows! That's why they crossed the river, that's why they are coming back. Oh, that murderer! If he ever falls into my hands! As I said, you must leave me and go on ahead. I'll settle accounts with him."

"Enough of that, Bai Nestor!" my brother interrupted sharply. "The important thing is how to get out of here as quickly as possible. By some chance they haven't discovered us yet. But if we delay . . . no, whether we're ready or not, we're leaving tonight. Oh, why didn't I buy that other camel!" He banged his fist in annoyance. "And we ought to have got in more food!"

"I brought a few things," said El Shakhin, pointing to the sacks he had dumped on the floor. "Anyway, we still have time until tonight. No one is looking for me."

"But how will we cross over to the other bank?" asked Lilliah, timidly breaking into the conversation.

"There are all the boats you could want along the river bank," I said. "We saw them last night. We could take one."

"Rali is right," Lukan agreed. "There is no problem about finding a boat. But we won't be able to handle it. The river is high and there is a strong current. We'll have to hire someone."

"I can handle a boat."

"El Shakhin, you are . . ."

"Wait! Wait!" I burst out, sitting up in my excitement over the sudden thought that had struck me. "I know the best solution."

"What is it, Rali?"

Before beginning, I looked at each of them in turn. I felt that it was the only thing that could save us, but I wanted to consider it carefully first.

"Tell us what it is."

"Lukan, you want us to get across to the other bank, right?"

"Well, are we to stay here for ever?"

"Nonsense! Really you don't understand a thing, Bate . . ."

"All right, all right. The teacher doesn't understand; the

pupil does. Let's hear what you have to say."

"Don't make fun of me! We must go south."

"There's no water to the south," El Shakhin echoed his words of a few days earlier.

"Yes there *is* water to the south, El Shakhin. We're by the river, aren't we?"

"But we can't keep beside the river all the way, Rali! It goes on for hundreds of miles! There are mountains, ravines . . ."

"We can, El Shakhin! Not beside the river but *on* the river!"

"By boat, you mean? But what about the animals? Where would we put them? No, I'm not in favor of this idea, arkadashlar."

"Be patient, El Shakhin," Lukan said. "I'm beginning to see what Rali is driving at. You're thinking of the Greek's boat, aren't you?"

"Yes," I nodded.

He was silent for a moment, knitting his blond eyebrows in thought, his beard quivering in excitement.

"But Kyr Lambros will give us away," he said at last. "Or, supposing we pay him as far as Feludjah, then if he tells Feisal Bey, he'll say we are going to Feludjah. And what is to stop us from getting off before Feludjah? There are two boatmen— we'll persuade them, or we'll force them, if necessary, to let us off where we want. Even if Feisal Bey finds out somehow, by then we will be far away. Do you all agree?" he asked.

"We agree!" the four of us chanted.

"Actually, it is not Rali who should say he agrees, but I," Lukan said with a smile. "And I must admit, this time the pupil taught his teacher something."

I knew that he said this to please me, because I was injured and because he was fond of me, and my whole face flushed with embarrassment.

"You've humiliated him, Lukan!"

"No, Bai Nestor! I didn't humiliate him. Making this admission is the least I can do to reward him."

Chapter 17

Father Euphrates

KYR LAMBROS' BOAT WAS LARGE, WITH A FLAT
bottom and a single wide sail, which caught the fair wind
and filled out nicely.

We settled ourselves at the front in the bash,* under an
awning of sturdy matting. At night we tilted the awning at a
sharper angle, so that we would be protected from the cold
current of air which sometimes hit us when we turned a bend.
In the daytime it shielded us from the hot sun.

Kyr Lambros had given instructions for the cargo of kegs
and bales to be covered with large mats. The after-part of the
boat, where the helm was situated, was entirely strewn with
these dirty black coverings. Mustapha, one of the two boatmen,
a swarthy Kurd with a bristly mop of hair and a bare torso,
who was a little older than I, would scramble over them all
day long and I was amazed that he did not break a leg.
Nowadays I looked mostly at people's legs. At places there
was no support under the matting and it often caved in beneath
his weight, sending him sprawling.

At the helm stood the second boatman, Liazim-Baba, a Sudanese. Old, wrinkled and as black as charcoal, he spoke in such a loud voice that his every word carried to the furthest corner of the boat. If he happened to pass me (I was always lying under the awning), Liazim-Baba would stop, squat on his heels and start telling me stories about the sprites that flitted over the water at night or ran races, riding on the backs of winged fishes.

As I watched the tall shifting banks that had a sameness about them, yet varied slightly every second, I could not help sensing that something unusual was going on around me or, rather, around Lilliah, for she was sitting, as usual, under the awning not far away. In their conversations, which for want of any other occupation had grown endless, she and Lukan were joined more and more often by El Shakhin, and by the high-spirited young Kurd, Mustapha. Sometimes Liazim-Baba would fasten the tiller and come over too, but he would merely squat on his heels and gaze in speechless admiration at the girl or, if he chanced to make a remark or explain a point, for he had sailed the river dozens of times, his voice would echo throughout the boat and drown the endless lapping and swishing of the waves that had been with us ever since we left Rakka.

Naturally I, too, would join in their conversations. It is not like me to keep quiet, and I must confess that I have my opinion about everything and like to give it. But since I had been wounded there were times when I felt depressed and gloomy. I spent more time watching and listening than talking, and I was more inclined to brood than join in the discussions. It was not just that alone. A sort of lethargy had come over me. I thought to myself, wherever we are carried by the tide and the wind, and no matter what awaits us there, we cannot complain for the time being. A calm, deceptive perhaps, had settled on us and we had nothing to do but regain our strength, look at the scenery and talk.

"How high the banks are here!" Lilliah remarked in her lilting voice towards the evening of the second day, turning her head first to the right and then to the left.

The men sitting round her all looked up, and so did I.

At this point the river narrowed to a mere hundred or a hundred and fifty paces in width. I could clearly distinguish not only the sheer white cliffs, eroded in countless places by the water, but also the long, dark, dangling roots of the tamarisks which bloomed, pink and mauve, along the edge of the bank, their roots screening the cavernous holes made by the river, like the beaded curtains of a barber's shop. There was a flurry of wings as a flock of wild ducks rose in the air. From far away came the piercing cry of an unfamiliar animal. All this, combined with the fresh smell of the lapping water, with the sky, pale as the chalk of the cliffs, with the flapping of the sail that billowed over our heads, all this was so different from the cheerless scene we had been faced with until just a few days ago that we could not take our eyes from it and kept uttering exclamations that were quite inadequate to express our feelings.

"What a riot of beauty!" gasped Lukan.

And the gay, boisterous Mustapha turned lustrous eyes on Lilliah and started to sing:

> Have you already forgotten me
> Or did you never know me,
> Lady of the roses,
> Fragrance of the roses. . . .

"We sing that song too," said El Shakhin, with a sigh, and I could not help noticing that his face and his whole body contracted with the spasm of pain I now knew so well.

More deeply moved than ever before, he could not refrain from joining in the song. His voice was neither as clear nor as powerful as Mustapha's, but it vibrated with tenderness and feeling in every note. He sang looking deliberately away from us, gazing straight ahead into the distance where the banks seemed to draw together into a narrow gorge. We listened in silence to the duet of the two voices that chased and soared in youthful lament:

Do you no longer see me
Or have you never seen me,
Lady of the roses,
Fragrance of the roses. . . .

No, there was no doubt about it; the taciturn El Shakhin
had fallen in love with Bai Nestor's daughter, fallen in love
like my brother and was suffering deeply and painfully, you
could tell from the way he sang.

This discovery upset me.

What about her? I looked at her. She had turned to face
my brother and was gazing into his eyes with such tenderness
and happiness that instead of being reassured I grew still more
uneasy. Wouldn't El Shakhin feel bitter towards them?
Wouldn't he start hating us all and eventually do us some
harm, even though our common fate had held us together so
far? I was young, but I remembered more than one case of
this kind in Panagyurishte. My mother, too, God rest her, used
to tell of them.

The song came to an end and El Shakhin sat motionless
for a long time, looking into the distance. But the lively Kurd
could not sit in one place for long. He jumped up, placed his
hands on either side of his mouth like a megaphone and, for
no apparent reason, started shouting at the top of his voice.

"Hallooo! Here we are! It's us! We're going from Rakka
to Feludjah!"

"Who are you shouting at?" asked Lukan curiously. "Are
there any houses up there?"

"No, there's nothing," Mustapha replied with a grin.

"Well then?"

"I always shout like this."

"That's all right, I've no objection."

"I shout. The Sudanese taught me. Tell them, Liazim-Baba!"

"That's how," said the black boatman. "Much shout—good!
Much not shout—bad!"

"But why?" we asked in bewilderment. "What is good and
what is bad about it?"

"That's how," said the old Sudanese, flashing his teeth and
spreading his large hands in an exaggerated gesture of help-

lessness. "Man alone shout. Many people—no shout!"

"Aha! I begin to understand."

"I think I have an inkling too, Lukan," Bai Nestor said with a nod, adding in Bulgarian, "It must be something like being in prison. When there are plenty of people, time passes more quickly. A man alone goes mad if he doesn't shout."

"You know, fellows, I've always been meaning to ask you, what language are you talking?" Mustapha broke in. "I heard you yesterday and again this morning. You are Christians, but you aren't Greeks. And you aren't Armenians either!"

We exchanged glances. Actually there was no reason to keep it a secret—we had already decided that.

"We are Bulgarians, Mustapha."

"Bulgarians? What are they?"

"Well, look at us," I said, eyeing him derisively. Imagine a good-for-nothing Kurd asking me in that tone of voice what Bulgarians were. The idea! I was about to tell him all about our kings, and how Constantinople had trembled at our approach, but my brother forestalled me.

"The Bulgarians are a people like any other, Mustapha. They're a Slavic people. We are about as numerous as the Greeks."

"Ah, that means just as many!"

But did he really know how many Greeks there were or was he judging by the number he had encountered at Rakka and Feludjah?

"And where is it? Where's your country?" he persisted curiously.

"Our country is a long way off, Mustapha. You know where Constantinople is, don't you?" asked my brother, feeling it was his turn to question. After all, he was not a geography teacher for nothing!

"I have a vague idea."

"Well, if you go north from Constantinople and then west up to the Danube, the whole of that territory is Bulgaria, or Bulgaristan in Turkish."

"But what is that Danube you mentioned?"

"A river, Mustapha! A big river! Twice as large as your Father Euphrates."

"No! Twice as large? You're joking!"

"It's true, Mustapha."

"What was its name again? Don . . . Dan . . ."

"Danube, Mustapha. You Moslems call it Tuna."

"Tuna? Ah, I seem to have heard that name somewhere. That's right, I've heard say there is such a river."

He flashed a look of astonishment at my brother. "Just a minute! That war, the war we are going to fight against the Muscovite . . . it's because of you then! I've heard about it, now I remember."

"That is an entirely different matter," my brother replied. "We know nothing about that. My brother and I are merchants. We are selling razors."

"Razors?"

"Razors, Mustapha. But I'll tell you what happened. We came to see these friends of ours on business. They live in these parts. But we were attacked by robbers and everything went wrong."

There was certainly something wrong with his story, and anyone instead of this young Kurd would easily have spotted it, but he merely waved a hand.

"Ah well," he said, "there are all sorts of people in the world. Some do business, some earn their living by robbery, others decide we must go to war."

"Yes, there are those too."

"If they are so eager, let them go! For my part, arkadash, I want nothing to do with the war. If you want to know, I won't go even if they force me."

He saw astonishment in our faces and immediately told us his secret.

"I have decided," he said, with a proud glance at Lilliah, "I have quite made up my mind now. As soon as we deliver the cargo at Feludjah, I shall quit the boat and the Greek and go to Baghdad. I have an uncle in Baghdad who has two shops. I've decided to go into business myself. Those who want to fight can go ahead!"

Well, that was one way of looking at it. Listening to him I was reminded of my friend Abu Talib and of the conversation he had had with the agalar of Diyarbakir on the evening the newspaper announced that war was imminent. The same faith, but what different people! I desperately wanted to believe that humanity would triumph in the end, and that my Abu Talib had not only forgiven me the lies I had to tell him but also had understood and did not think ill of me.

And so we traveled for another three days, faster in some stretches of the river, more slowly in others. At first we did not stop for the night, but when the river widened and grew shallower, we would cast anchor at some sheltered point along the bank when the sun set, and sleep over until the following morning.

Several times our boat, despite its flat bottom, stuck in the mud of the riverbed and incredible efforts were needed to dislodge it with the help of long poles. Once the sharp points of underwater rocks appeared suddenly in mid-stream, ringed with foam from the waves, and only the skill of the seasoned Liazim-Baba saved us from a terrible disaster. Often the river would be split by narrow sandbars, where flocks of gulls and martins would pause for a rest. The irrepressible Mustapha amused himself by taking potshots at them with his long rusty pistol. The birds would quickly fly away, filling the air with their sharp, startled cries.

Occasionally we would even sail past some island, overgrown with wild vegetation. The wind would bring us the scent of flowers, the aroma of resin. At such moments I would be seized with a strong urge to leap ashore, plunge into the undergrowth and roll in the lush grass. But there was no sense in stopping. Besides, the painful thought struck me that I could not even stand up. The wound in my shoulder was healing rapidly, but that seemingly minor injury had made my leg swell and took up all my attention.

The river had grown wider and then shallower, because of the terrain. As the days passed, the banks grew further apart and diminished in height. The white chalk cliffs disappeared and the desert frequently gave way to vast expanses of steppe. Now and then we would see a straggling herd of goats or a long file of swaying camels. The flatness of the land was relieved by little groves of date-palms. We also came across stray Bedouin tents and the round clay houses of sedentary tribes.

We even passed a couple of landing stages, where the men and children waved greetings to us.

Mustapha was not slow to respond. "Hallooo!" he bawled. "It's us! It's us! We're going from Rakka to Feludjah!" Or he would ask, "Has the Hunchback been along? Eh? The Hunchback?"

"Who is the Hunchback?" I finally inquired. "Is he a friend of yours? Is he going to Feludjah too?"

Mustapha rocked with laughter. "There isn't any Hunchback," he said with a wink.

"What do you mean? If there isn't any, then why do you ask about him?"

"Oh, just for something to do! And to give them something to think about!"

And he scampered over the matting to set the sail straight. Just then a rumbling sound came from the helm. It rose and swelled and soon began to resemble a song.

Liazim-Baba was singing. But he was singing in his own strange tongue. Only the melancholy refrain told us that he was probably thinking of his African homeland, from which he had been taken goodness knows how many years ago, and to which he would probably never return.

As I sat and listened, I was filled with pity and sorrow. Why was the world made like that, I wondered sadly. Will it always be like that? Beside me under the awning, Lukan, Bai Nestor and El Shakhin were talking quietly. What about? I did not listen. My eyes were fastened on the huge waterwheel projecting from the left bank to catch the flow of the river. It was one of those odd contrivances for drawing water that we were meeting more and more often, and which filled the silence with their interminable creaking and splashing. Truly ingenious! I examined it with growing curiosity, remembering that at home they harnessed blind horses or patient donkeys for that purpose. But how much water could an animal draw? Hardly enough to irrigate the desert! Here the fellaheen* had harnessed the river itself for the job. A stone wall ran inland from the river's edge, and large wooden wheels, with slender pitchers suspended from them, revolved within its open arches. The flow of water pushed up the pitchers, which tilted over and spilt the accumulated water into a large trough, attached to the top of the stone wall. From there it flowed into narrow ditches dug in the ground, which carried the water through the fields and gardens, large and plentiful in these parts.

"They ought to set up wheels like that at home, all along the Maritsa and everywhere!" I cried excitedly.

My brother glanced at the wheel, gave me a nod, as if to say that he agreed, and returned to his conversation.

I was taken aback by this and started to listen.

"He said we would reach Salahieh tomorrow."

Was "he" Mustapha or the Sudanese? Anyway, Salahieh meant as much to me as Mayadin, which we had passed.

"Salahieh, Abu-Kemal, I know those places, arkadashlar," the Syrian said, nodding. "Yes, I am for Salahieh too! From there we can go straight to Palmyra, then to Homs, and on to Tripoli."

"Still a long road to travel, boys," Bai Nestor said with a shake of his head.

"Long but glorious," said my brother and gave him an encouraging smile.

"Very well then, Salahieh it shall be! We'll tell them that we've decided to get off there."

"We could even slip away during the night without any fuss."

"They'd notice us, El Shakhin. Besides, even if we do slip away, they'll think something has happened to us. They might alert the authorities. It would be better to tell them that we've decided to go back to Deir-es-Sor. We'll ask them to let us off at Salahieh, pretending that we are taking a boat back from there."

"That's a clever idea, Lukan. What do you say, El Shakhin?" asked Bai Nestor.

"I agree," said the Syrian shortly and, being suspicious of him now, I tried for a long time to detect any sign of treachery in his dark eyes.

* * * *

We were still a long way from Salahieh when something hit me in the face. It could not have been a mosquito, for they were light and there were hundreds of them. Anyway, by now I paid no attention to their buzzing. I fingered my cheek; it didn't itch. I felt about on the mattress. There was nothing there.

At that moment Lilliah called out, "What was that?"

"What was what?"

"I don't know—something hit me!"

"Me too!"

Suddenly a host of tiny grayish-green creatures started to flap around us and all over us—dozens, hundreds of them. No, thousands! The awning echoed like a drum as they thudded against it. "Locusts! Locusts!" we cried, amused at the surprise.

Then El Shakhin ran up, followed by Mustapha.

"Drive them away! Beat them off! Get them out of the boat!" they screamed in desperate alarm. Their fear of the little long-legged insects struck me as so absurd that I burst out laughing.

"Quick!" cried the Syrian, normally so impassive. "Mustapha, have you a shovel? A broom? Lukan! Throw them into the water or they'll smother us. They'll gnaw everything to bits."

I was speechless. Such a thought had not even occurred to me. And yet they really could smother us and gnaw away the ropes, for they were descending in such thick swarms, jostling and fighting to get onto the boat, that wherever I looked the air was green with them.

"Everyone hold tight!" boomed the voice of the pilot, Liazim-Baba. "Watch boat. Whoops!"

And, indeed, the boat suddenly began to rock, heeled over, thrashed about and finally came to rest with its broad sail slanting in the direction of the oncoming swarm. The locusts crashed into the sail and fell, sliding down the awning, which the agile Mustapha promptly tilted still more. Then Lilliah and I, sitting beneath it, saw a sight that few can have witnessed before. As if a floodgate had been opened, an endless stream of locusts poured onto the bow in front of us, a gray-green, quivering, jumping hoard, which Mustapha and El Shakhin, one with a wooden oar and one with a broom of stout twigs, kept shoveling and sweeping into the river. But where were Lukan and Bai Nestor? I could hear my brother's

voice somewhere nearby, Balyu's frantic barking and the re-
sounding bellows of the camels.

Oh, why did I have to be such an invalid! Why wasn't my
leg in better shape! I could have wept aloud.

How long the extraordinary battle lasted I cannot say for
sure. Certainly not more than a few minutes. When it was
over and the boat resumed its course with its bow facing forward, everywhere I looked were squashed, fluttering and jumping insects.

"Phew!" El Shakhin mopped his face. "And Rali thought
it was going to be fun!"

"Imagine being so afraid of those tiny little creatures!" I
forced a smile. "We should have taken them along to Feludjah,
that's all. If Kyr Lambros finds out that we've done him out of
some extra profit . . ."

As I was speaking, up came the Sudanese. He looked at the
sky and shook his head unhappily. "Not good," he said.

"It's all over, Liazim-Baba," my brother assured him, pat-
ting him on the back. "Thanks to you we escaped. To tell the
truth, like Rali, I thought it was all rather a joke at first."

"No, effendi. Still very bad!"

"What do you mean *still?* More locusts?"

The Sudanese looked at the sky. "No, no. Oof! Sun is hot!"

"I'll say. It's as hot as a furnace," I agreed.

Liazim-Baba kept shaking his head. "Hot—oof! But locusts,
effendi? So many locusts! Why here? Why on river? Why on
boat?"

"Maybe it was on their way," I remarked and everyone
laughed, except the Sudanese.

"Very bad," he said and started back to his helm.

"Try and figure him out," said Bai Nestor with a grimace.

My brother made no reply. It was clear that he did not
understand either. El Shakhin took the broom and began to
sweep out the bow. Lilliah went to help him, but I could see
that her assistance embarrassed the Syrian. He handed her the
broom in silence and went off to the back of the boat where
Mustapha was picking up the mats that covered the merchandise
and shaking them over the water.

My brother and Bai Nestor gazed at the low bare banks

ahead and talked together in undertones about the next landing. What would we find at Salahieh? Would we be able to buy three more camels there? And what would they cost us? Our funds were getting dangerously low, and we had to save enough for the steamer to Tripoli.

"Oh, baaad!" came another wail from the Sudanese.

Poor Liazim-Baba has been unhinged by the locusts, I thought. Or perhaps one of his water sprites in the stories he had told me had given him a fright. From my reclining position, I cast a fleeting glance at the sky. In the west it was clear and bright. But over the eastern bank the horizon was darkened by a dense mass of blue-black cloud that appeared to be as heavy as iron. Was that what Liazim-Baba had meant by "bad"?

"Look!" I cried. "Bate! Bai Nestor!"

"What's the matter, Rali?" Both of them, however, had followed my gaze and the old man uttered a gasp of dismay.

"How could he have known?" he groaned. "How on earth? From the locusts, that's it. He realized that the storm was driving them this way. Since it was driving them, the storm was bound to come this way too. But there's no point in talking about it. Mustapha! Here, Mustapha! Steer for the shore. There's a storm heading this way."

"The shore is too level here, effendi. We'll have to find a cove."

"Look, over there! There's an island on the left. We can shelter behind it."

"Liazim-Baba!" we heard Mustapha call. "Make for the lee side of the island!"

"Island far away, trouble close," the Sudanese replied.

Indeed, even before the boat started to head towards the sheltering island, somewhere up among the clouds, which were creeping menacingly towards the sun, there was a rumble of thunder. The air turned heavy and sultry. There was still no wind, but the water around the boat started to rise and fall rhythmically.

All at once it was dark. I looked up and saw that the sun had gone.

"It's starting to rain," said Lukan. "Lilliah, get under the awning."

Sure enough, the first big heavy drops were starting to patter down on the matting, reminding me of the arrival of the locusts.

"It's quite true, quite true, as they say, troubles never come singly."

"Never mind about troubles, Bai Nestor. See if the camels are safely tied up. Rali, call Balyu. And you, Lilliah, get further under that awning, and put on something warm."

While rapping out instructions in his usual efficient way, my brother was moving the sacks of food, weapons and gunpowder to a safer place.

"El Shakhin! Where are you, man?"

"I am helping Mustapha take down the sail."

"How will we get to the island then?"

"We won't get there. We must abandon ourselves to the will of Allah, arkadash," El Shakhin replied.

It was certainly senseless to imagine that we could reach the island. The whole sky was black now, and closing in on us. It grew dark as night and we could hardly see one another. The thunderclouds chased and rolled overhead until, suddenly, the whole expanse was lit up by a blinding flash and we were jolted by a deafening explosion. For a moment a bottomless, terrifying silence reigned.

Then the rain came pelting down, a howling, swirling wind swept us off our feet, and the waves tossed the boat and flooded the decks. We stared in terror at each other's ghostly white faces as a mighty crash rent the sky. Boom! echoed the horizons. Then rain and more rain . . .

"Are you holding on to each other? Have you tied yourselves to the mast?" roared my brother, grabbing me with one hand and flinging the other round Lilliah and the mast. "Bai Nestor, are you holding on?"

"I'm holding on, Lukan. Oh, Lord, what we've been through! If only the boat doesn't overturn! Let's just hope we don't hit something."

Our boat spun around in the seething waves. Liazim-Baba had either taken shelter or had been swept away by the hurricane. And where was El Shakhin? What had happened to Mustapha?

Just then the whole boat seemed to rise into the air, and then
—plop! We were falling, sinking . . .

"We've overturned. Oh, Lord! Lilliah! My child!"

"Father! Lukan!"

"Bate!" I shrieked.

"Be brave, we won't overturn! Keep calm!" shouted Lukan.
His voice, so harsh and frightening at that moment, reassured
us more than any display of tenderness.

We did not overturn. We were saved by the flat bottom of
the boat. Then we were caught up by another wave, tossed to
and fro, dragged up to the crest and hurled with tremendous
force. The boat hit something solid, toppled over, scattering us
in all directions. I rolled over and over, and bumped my bad
leg so hard against the side of the boat that I cried out in pain.

"Where are you all? Rali! Lilliah!" I heard my brother call.

Again came the howling wind. We no longer rocked in
response. Battered though it might be, the boat had run aground
somewhere and we were safe.

"Unload everything quickly. Unload, or the boat will drift
back!" my brother shouted.

"We'll tie boat, tie it fast. Here, rocks! Ropes, Mustapha!
Hurry!"

Liazim-Baba passed close by, and even bent down to inquire
about hanim-effendi,* but he was so black that I could not see
him in the dark.

"Bate! Is anyone hurt? Where's Balyu? Are you there,
Balyu?"

Lilliah had sprained her wrist. El Shakhin had grazed his
neck. Otherwise everyone was all right.

"Where are we? Which bank are we on?" I asked of Lukan,
as he carried me off the boat, with Balyu yapping and whimper-
ing beside us.

"I don't know yet, Rali. The main thing is that we are safe."

Chapter 18

The Last Encounter

WHEN THE STORM HAD PASSED AND THE SUN SHONE again, dazzlingly bright as usual, we were overjoyed to find that we had been swept right over to the bank we had planned to land on. According to Liazim-Baba, the little town of Salahieh was still some distance away, and we were cut off from it by a massive mountain range. So, after we had helped our new-found friends to push the boat back onto the river, we said goodbye to them, wished them a good journey to Feludjah, and struck off inland into the desert, where El Shakhin hoped to find more than one oasis.

Once again luck was on our side. Our companion in mis-fortune found not only the oases he had promised us but also some good friends there. This made it easier for us to continue the journey. And, by the time we reached Syria itself, we found gardens, vineyards and fields all around us.

El Shakhin thought that we should go still further south, even beyond Damascus, where a whole district was controlled by tribes that had risen against the Turks. We could be his guests there until our pursuers had forgotten all about us. But quite frankly, in spite of everything El Shakhin had done for us, I still harbored traces of fear and suspicion towards him. So I was very quick to support Lukan when he said, "We are grateful for the invitation, dear El Shakhin, but, like you, we are longing to be home. They are preparing for war there now —a war for freedom! For five hundred years the people have been waiting for this war. How can we stay here at such a time?"

"We are going to Tripoli," I added. "Once we get there, things will be easier. We talked about it, remember? There is a merchant there. Hedi Zegal is his name. My friend Abu Talib said we should go to him. He'll find us a ship bound for home."

"In that case," said the Syrian, "I'll go with you."

"Don't do that, El Shakhin. Why should you?" we protested.

Even Lilliah spoke up. "You would do better to go to your family and make them happy. You must have parents, a wife . . ."

"No, I have no wife," said El Shakhin, and quickly changed the subject. "Think it over," he continued. "You say that this Hedi Zegal of yours is a merchant? What if he happens to be out of town?"

We exchanged glances. He was right—what if the merchant was out of town?

"We'll manage somehow," Lukan said confidently.

"No, arkadash, I'm coming with you. I have a cousin at Tripoli, a first cousin. I know that at one time he had a boat, like Liazim-Baba. And a big boat too!"

We were unable to dissuade him and he set off with us.

One morning four days later, after we had crossed the high Lebanese mountains (how wonderfully the huge cedars smelt of resin! And everything seemed to be saying soon, very soon, Rali, you will be seeing your mountains and forests), we found ourselves approaching the walls of a little seaport. Beyond it lay the blue of the sea.

"There is your Tripoli," said El Shakhin, pointing to the walls. "But now comes the bad part. To enter, you need passes.

That is the practice here. Strangers are asked for their passes. But I can go in."

"But you're not from here! They don't know you!"

"No, I am not," he conceded. "But I am an Arab. Don't you remember what it was like at Rakka? At the gates they ask you in Arabic where you are going and whom you are looking for."

He was right; we certainly had not foreseen that problem.

"Listen, my friend," my brother began. His pale eyebrows were drawn together over his nose, and a thick blue vein throbbed at his temples. "This is what you must do," he went on, after a moment's hesitation. "Tell the merchant Hedi Zegal that you were sent by someone who knows Abu Talib of Diyarbakir. But don't tell him that we are Christians. Be on your guard in any case! Let him come to us. We'll be waiting for him."

He turned and thoughtfully surveyed the landscape for a while. The vine and myrtle-clad mountain slopes ended in a steep cliff at the sea. Where *could* we wait? It was dangerous here near the gates.

"I know these parts," said El Shakhin. "The best place is over on that promontory. It is covered with bushes. People seldom go there and there are some steps cut into the rock. You can go down to the sea that way if necessary. I mean, if I find my cousin, I'll get him to take me there with the boat."

There was no alternative. Anyway, El Shakhin's suggestion was a sensible one and we promptly agreed to it. He set off for the town while the four of us made for the green mountain slope that jutted out into the sea.

Strange how one will start out for a destination full of hope and confidence, without the slightest suspicion of what awaits one there!

The spot where we settled down to wait was convenient and sheltered. A wet salt breeze blew up from the sea, bringing relief from the heat. From below came the steady roar and the thudding of the surf against the cliff.

We arranged our clothing as best we could, winding turbans round our heads to look like Moslems, and prepared to wait for Hedi Zegal.

But Bai Nestor and his daughter sat near the edge of the

➤ 215

cliff. I lay between the two camels, stroking Balyu with my good hand. Lukan was ostensibly cleaning his revolver and loading it, but I noticed that his eyes kept seeking Lilliah's.

"Lilliah, child, sing me something to remind me of the old days," said Bai Nestor suddenly.

"You know I don't feel like singing, father," she replied.

Bai Nestor said nothing. He shifted his rifle to the other side and gazed first out to sea and then back to where, far away beyond the mountains and the deserts, we had left a black fortress and a lonely grave.

"When you were only very small, just so high," he held his hand a few feet above the ground, "your mother always used to sing you this song. How did it go? 'Little bird, little bird, where is your nest?' "

"Oh, I remember! That's right," and she began to hum softly.

"I have no nest, but I have a heart . . ."

Bai Nestor gave a sob, wiped his eyes and was silent for a long time.

"Now there will be a nest for you too, Lilliah," he said finally. "Wait till you see how beautiful our country is, our Bulgaria."

"Bul-ga-ri-a!" she repeated softly. Then a thought occurred to her and she looked at Lukan. Meeting his eyes she suddenly flushed scarlet.

I was curious, but I also felt a little uncomfortable watching them, so I turned my eyes to the sea.

A large ship, with its sail full spread, was approaching the shore. A tall man, stripped to the waist, was at the helm. Another man, wearing a white veil, was standing in the bow of the boat. He was gazing towards our cliff and waving.

"Isn't that El Shakhin?" I cried joyfully.

Lukan jumped up instantly. "That's him! And the other man must be his cousin."

The boat drew nearer and nearer.

"Lukan! Bai Nestor!" I heard El Shakhin shout from below. "Come down quickly! Hurry!"

"What?" called my brother, his hands to his mouth like a funnel.

"Come down . . . Hedi Zegal is a traitor . . . I only just escaped from Feisal Bey!"

Feisal Bey! We hadn't expected to hear any more of him. Who had told him we were here? That we were looking for Hedi Zegal? That we wanted him to find us a ship?

"Who? Your Abu Talib, of course!" Lukan declared, suddenly turning to me. "It's all up! Hurry!"

"No—it can't be true!" I made a last attempt to defend my benefactor.

At that moment Balyu jumped up, let out a growl and then started barking furiously.

"The search party!" yelled Bai Nestor. "Lilliah! Go down quickly. Lukan, take Rali!"

It was so terrifyingly sudden—the collapse of all our hopes!

The zaptiehs were still hidden by the bushes, but we could already hear the hoofbeats of their horses.

"You are coming with us!" my brother ordered.

"Someone has to hold them back. Give me your revolvers." Bai Nestor snatched them out of his hands. "At least they're loaded, thank goodness!"

"Bai Nestor!"

"Go on! Get away. Save them, at least. Lilliah, child. Goodbye, my child. Goodbye!" He clasped her fiercely to him.

"Father!"

"Go . . . go with him. Goodbye, Lukan, my friend. Take care of her. Rali . . . Lilliah, my dearest . . . Goodbye . . ."

Now we could actually see the zaptiehs. They must have seen us too, for they jumped from their horses, took cover behind the bushes and started crawling towards us.

We could not stay there any longer. With a stony face, drained of all color, my brother lifted me onto his shoulder. I whistled to Balyu and, with Lilliah, we started to descend the steps in the face of the rock.

Before we were even out of sight, I heard Feisal Bey shout, "I'm going to catch you alive . . . alive! I'm going to throttle you with my own hands!"

"Come on, come on, murderer!" Bai Nestor called back. Then turning to us, he said, "Go, children . . . go on. You have a job to do."

Suddenly a shot rang out. But who fired it? Was Bai Nestor hit?

"Go on, quickly, Lilliah!" My brother hurried her along, but she kept stopping to listen, as if she did not understand what was happening.

Finally, we reached the shore. El Shakhin took me and carried me onto the boat, while Lukan helped Lilliah on board.

Up above the shots had ceased. Had Bai Nestor been killed? No. There he was, standing erect. How long his beard was, and his hair, blowing in the wind. Who was that going up to him? I strained to see. A short, thick-set man, charging like a bull. "Feisal Bey! Feisal Bey!" I repeated aloud. He is going to carry out his threat. He is going to catch him alive!

Alive! At once, the two of them went for each other, started grappling. Which was the stronger? Oh! Bai Nestor took a step back . . . another . . . Stop! That's the edge of the cliff! But he didn't stop. He dragged Feisal Bey towards him with all his might, and the two of them went hurtling over the precipice. And I knew from Lilliah's terrible scream that it was not a dream.

The Ending of This Sad Story and the beginning of another, Which Shall Remain Untold

WE HAD TO ENDURE MANY MORE HARDSHIPS AS THE boat, on which we embarked for our long voyage, was buffeted from wave to wave. And we faced more than one peril as we skirted the Greek islands and sailed along the shores of the Peloponnese and Albania into the Adriatic.

All these troubles passed and were forgotten, but my disappointment in Abu Talib and the death of Bai Nestor left their mark on me.

Sometimes, as the east wind filled out the sail of the boat and the sea gulls circled about the mast, I would relive the whole story of our escape, my mind going back to poor Meira and her evil master. Then my thoughts would invariably turn to Abu Talib. I would tell myself: he was fond of me, he helped me, then he went and betrayed me. Why? Because he found out I was not of his faith? Abu Talib, Abu Talib—how long must men be divided by their beliefs and treat each other worse than beasts? You are not bad at heart, I never found you bad, and yet you, too, turned out to have some bad in you. How long? Look at El Shakhin! Think what he had to overcome—religion, love . . . and now he is our brother.

At times like these I also thought of Bai Nestor. His Lilliah could now say whole sentences in Bulgarian. How could she help learning with such a teacher! But Bai Nestor, her father, had been left behind on the jagged rocks by the sea, locked in the arms of his mortal enemy. He would never, never return to his homeland.

Yes, there I was rocking on the waves, and on a sea of memories. My brother kept saying, "Put your memories behind you. Think of the present."

But I can't help it, that's the way I am. Anyway, even though memories are uppermost in my mind, I still have time for the present. And if he really wants to know, I even think about the future.

Early one morning we arrived at Venice. There all our sufferings came to an end.

With tears in our eyes we parted from our unforgettable El Shakhin and his cousin. We washed and changed our clothes, but there was no time to rest. We learned from the papers that Russia had finally declared war on Turkey and that she was moving her troops to the Danube.

That is what you might call good timing!

Two days before we left for Bucharest, where Lukan and I signed up as volunteers in the Bulgarian brigade, my brother and Lilliah were married in the local Russian church. I, naturally, was the kum.* And the kumitsa? We found one too, but that was much, much later.

When we arrived at Bucharest, Lilliah went to work as a nurse in one of the Russian military hospitals. Balyu also enlisted—in the volunteer brigade with us. As luck would have it, we all three found ourselves in the same company. Lukan was a corporal, I was a bugler and Balyu ran ahead to reconnoiter, since he already had some experience in that task. And what experience!

Soon we started for the south. Another southward journey! But this time we were not alone, and we were not weak. We were marching in step with great Russia. A great day had dawned at last for our long-suffering country, Bulgaria.

DICTIONARY

of Turkish, Bulgarian, Arabian, and Other Foreign Words

A

aga   (s.), sir   *agalar* (pl.), sirs, gentlemen   (Turkish)

Allah akbar   praise be to Allah!   (Turkish, Arabian)

arkadash   (s.), friend, comrade   (pl. *arkadashlar*)   (Turkish)

asper   smallest Turkish copper coin

B

babà   father   (Turkish)

bàba   old woman   (Bulgarian)

bash   bow of a boat   (Turkish)

bash-giaour   chief or head infidel   (Turkish)

bashi-bazouks   mercenaries of Turkish irregulars, notorious for pillage and brutality

bate   Bulgarian term used for addressing an older brother   (pronounced: BAH-teh)

bashi-bazouk

bey   governor of district in Turkish dominions; also title of respect, as for military or naval officers and others   (Arabian)

bey effendi   (or *efendi*), a double title of respect, mister governor (Turkish)

boza   a non-alcoholic drink made of millet, which is a small-seed cereal; a millet ale   (Turkish)

bozadji   a seller of *boza*   (Turkish, Bulgarian, Persian)

boza-seller

C

caftan   man's long tunic or gown, having long sleeves and fastened with a girdle   (Turkish, Persian, Arabian)

caique   a light skiff or rowboat; sometimes a small sailing vessel (Turkish)

caique

chalma   Turkish headdress, a man's turban

chibouk   long Turkish tobacco pipe

E

effendi   (or *efendi*), master, sir, mister; title of respect   (Turkish)

effendiler   (or *efendiler*), gentlemen (Turkish)

chibouk

F

fellaheen   (pl.), peasants in Egypt, Syria, and other Arabian-speaking countries   (s. *fellah*)

feredje   a large veil, a kind of shawl (Turkish)

fez   Turkish cap or headdress

G

giaour   infidel or non-Moslem (Turkish)

chalma

H

hadji   a Moslem who has made his hadji or pilgrimage to Mecca. Sometimes used as a title of respect, thus: Hadji Ali, that is, Pilgrim Ali   (Arabian, Turkish, Bulgarian)

haidouks   (or *haiduks*), bandit mountaineers or outlaws, especially those of the Balkan Slavs   (Greek, Bulgarian, Turkish)

fez

hanim-effendi   miss, title of respect for a young lady   (Turkish)

haremlik   women's quarters in a Turkish house

hookah	(also called *narghile* by Persians), a pipe with a flexible tube and attached vase of water through which smoke is drawn (Arabian)

hookah

I

Ingilizler	the English, Englishmen (Turkish)

K

kadina	(s.), woman (pl. *kadinas*) (Turkish)
kapia	gate (Turkish, Arabian)
kilometer	(or *kilometre*), 1,000 meters, or about ⅝ of a mile. Kilometer is a unit of length measurement in the metric system. (Example of modern made-up word from Old Greek words)
konak	Turkish government building
kum	(masc.) and *kumitsa* (fem.), sponsors, usually husband and wife, at an Orthodox wedding (Bulgarian)
kyr	mister (Greek)
kyrie	sir (Greek)

L

lira	a unit of money in Turkey and in Italy, a gold coin in the former and a silver coin in the latter country

M

muezzin	attendant in a mosque who calls Moslems to prayer from a minaret, five times a day (Arabian)
mutesarrif	(or *mutasarrif*), Turkish district governor

minaret with muezzin

N

Nejdee	(or *Nejdi*), a native or inhabitant of the kingdom of Nejd in Arabia. Nejdi horse, a breed of Arab horse from Nejd, noted for its speed and endurance.
nizam	regular soldiers in the Turkish armed forces

O

onbashi chief of police, usually in a small town   (Turkish)

P

padishah sultan, chief ruler, a great king, emperor. It was applied to the Shah of Persia, the Sultan of Turkey, and the Great Mogul of India.   (Persian)

pasha Turkish military, naval, or civil officer of high rank

pastrami cured (usually with pepper and spices) beef   (Arabian)

piaster (or *piastre*), coin, usually silver, of various countries, among them, Turkey, Rumania, Egypt, Syria, Italy   (Italian)

piazza place, square, marketplace in a town   (Italian)

pilaf (or *pilaff, pilau, pilaw*), Oriental dish of rice or cracked wheat, boiled with meat, fowl, fish, spices   (Persian, Turkish)

R

Rayahs non-Moslem Turkish subjects

S

salep hot, sweet, pungent drink (pictured here is a typical salep-seller)   (French,   Spanish, Arabian)

selamlik men's quarters in a Turkish house

sharlan walnut oil   (Turkish)

Y

yashmak a face-veil worn by Moslem women in public   (Turkish, Arabian)

yataghan long knife or short saber, without a crosspiece   (Turkish)

Z

zaptieh Turkish policeman

zourla musical instrument something like a clarinet   (Turkish)

salep-seller

yashmak

224 ◄